A Wellington Christmas

(A Wellington Cross Novella)

Cheryl R. Lane

Cheryl R Lane

ISBN: 1495912019
ISBN-13: 978-1495912016

Printed in the United States of America

This book is a work of fiction. The main characters in this story are fictional. The plantations mentioned are fictional, though inspired by the James River Plantations in Virginia. Some of the events in the story are based on factual events while others are products of the author's imagination.

Cover photo and author photo were taken by Sherrie Frontz.

Also by Cheryl R. Lane:

Wellington Cross (Book One in the Wellington Cross Series)
Wellington Grove (Book Two in the Wellington Cross Series)

One

December 1873
Williamsburg, Virginia

Ginny Brown started getting nauseous the first week of December. She knew what it could be, but she didn't want it to be. So she chose to ignore it. It could just be a germ she picked up at the academy.

She was attending nursing school at Williamsburg Female Academy. Her husband William drove her there by carriage in the mornings and then picked her up in the late afternoons after he was finished working in the clinic with Dr. Harrison. Some days, when he had to work late, she would start walking the three blocks back to their little cottage at the back of his Aunt Patsy's house, their temporary home for the next two years until she finished school to be a nurse and William finished his doctorate degree by working with the local doctor in clinical practice. Then they would go back to their new home which was being rebuilt in the forest between Wellington Cross and Magnolia Grove Plantations. Called The Forest by its original owners, the family of Thomas Jefferson's wife, it had been damaged, neglected for many years, and once William and Ginny found it, they started dreaming of a future together in it. It was there that they first declared their love for one another and where William presented her a beautiful engagement ring.

This night, on the streets of Williamsburg, the bells rang out at the Bruton Parish Church a few blocks away, and Ginny knew it was getting late. It was almost dark, and the torch lighter had already come by to light fresh pine logs in the high-reaching street baskets for the night. Ginny normally spent time after her last class of the day studying in the library on campus waiting for William, but he was later than usual today, and as the campus needed to lock up, she'd had to leave. She decided to go on and start walking home, taking the shortest route, which unfortunately meant she had to walk past the blacksmith shop where Samuel Bowen worked as an apprentice.

Sam had asked her to marry him last May at the same time she began courting William. She had no desire to court or marry Sam, and after he got violent with her, William came to her rescue, and between him and her step-father, Jonas Chambers, they forced him to leave the plantation. That had been the night of her cotillion ball, which turned out being an engagement ball, for William had proposed to her out by the river just after sunset, and she'd said yes. She'd been smitten with him since she was ten, and once he came back to the plantation after medical school, they fell in love and had a short engagement.

She tied her books up with a buckled leather strap and started walking, her nausea subsided for the moment. As she got closer to the blacksmith shop, she began to get a little nervous. She hardly ever saw Sam any more, but on occasion they would see each other from a distance but not talk. This night, he was outside at the side of the blacksmith shop hammering away. She thought about crossing the street to avoid him, but before she could do so, he looked up and met her eyes. It would be rude now to cross the street. Not that she cared if she was rude to him. He'd slapped her twice and lied to her countless times before, but she made a promise to William that if she were to run into him, she would be cordial. Their reputation as a newly married couple and his future in becoming a respected doctor depended on them both having outstanding reputations and good standing in the community. Even here in Williamsburg, though they would be moving back to Charles City County to start their careers.

And so, she did not cross the street but smiled and waved pleasantly at Sam.

He tipped his hat to her and stared at her as she kept walking. "It's a little late for you to be out walking in the dark, don't you think, *Mrs. Brown*?"

"Hello, Mr. Bowen. How nice to see you. Yes, it is getting late, but Mr. Brown should be coming down the road any time now."

Sam wiped his brow while still holding the hammer. "It's awfully cold out here. Why don't you go inside and visit with mother by the fire and have a cup of tea and some gingerbread – she made some just this afternoon. She has wanted to speak with you for some time now. I'll hail William down for you when he passes by."

Ginny hesitated for a moment. She looked in the upstairs window above the shop where Sam and his mother lived, noting that candles had been lit and placed in the windowsill, a Williamsburg Christmas tradition, along with wreaths decorated with fruit on all the doors. The warmth of being inside was tempting, as she was only wearing a shawl. It had been warm that morning, but the temperature had turned bitterly cold by the time she finished her classes. A nice cup of hot tea sounded wonderful, and her stomach gurgled at the thought of gingerbread.

She didn't exactly want to see Adaline Bowen, however. She'd been avoiding the woman ever since she had admitted to lying for her son in an effort to move into Magnolia Grove Plantation by getting her to marry Sam. They both told Ginny and her family that Sam owned his own blacksmith shop and that they still lived in their big house that Sam grew up in, when in fact, they'd lost their house and Sam was only an apprentice. It was William who helped them to get out of the boarding house they were living in and to move into the living quarters above the shop. Ginny didn't know what to say to Adaline, and yet William's wish that she be cordial with everyone nagged the back of her mind.

But she didn't think William would want her going inside the blacksmith shop with Sam there on the property. He could be lying again. Adaline could be out, as well as the owner of the shop, Mr. Holmes. If Sam was there alone, she could be putting herself in danger by going inside. No, she would not go in, as she could not trust Sam. As deceitful as he had been, he might not even hail William, as he said he would.

"That sounds nice, but I'm afraid I'll have to pass this time. Give her my regards," Ginny said politely and kept on walking.

She felt his eyes on the back of her head, but she kept going. As she got in front of the hat maker's shop, she heard a carriage turn down the street and turned around to see William in their carriage, pulled by his big black horse, Midnight, and her own tan horse, Buttercup. Her heart leapt, and she felt great relief and warmth at seeing him.

He stopped the carriage beside her and jumped down. She smiled at his handsome face, admiring the dark cropped beard that she talked him into keeping during the winter. After six months of marriage, he still took her breath away.

"Ginny, there you are!" He took her in a quick embrace.

"And here you are!" she said, hugging him tightly, shivering against his warm body.

"My darling, you're cold. I'm sorry to be so late. I was assisting Dr. Harrison in surgery, removing a gallbladder, and it took much longer than anticipated."

"It's all right. You're here now."

He rubbed his hands up and down her arms and then took her hands in his. "Your hands are like ice. Here, I have an early Christmas present for you," he said, his deep blue eyes sparkling with excitement.

"Oh, William, you shouldn't."

"Not another word. This is part of the reason I was late. I had to pick this up on the way over before the store closed."

He reached inside the carriage and pulled out a big long rectangular box.

"William, I don't need another dress," she protested.

"It's not a dress. Though, I'll have you know that if I wanted to buy you another dress, I would," he said, smirking. "I love spoiling you."

She smiled as he handed her the box.

"Open it up." He was practically dancing with anticipation.

"All right." She pried open the box to reveal a royal blue wool cape with big matching buttons and a high collar. Her eyes lit up. "Oh, William." She took it completely out of the box. It was long and very luxurious with a silk lining. "It's beautiful."

"Put it on." He helped her wrap it around and button the two buttons in front. "Perfect."

"It really is." It was very warm. There were two little slits for her hands, and she slipped her hands through and hugged him again. "Thank you. You're so thoughtful."

"When the weather turned cold this afternoon, I knew you didn't have on anything but a shawl and nothing much warmer than that here in Williamsburg, so I had the idea of getting you an early present. I went straight to your favorite dressmaker's shop, and sure enough, they had some capes hanging in the window display. I chose this color to match your eyes."

She wiped a tear creeping out of the corner of one of those very eyes and looked up at him adoringly. "I don't deserve you." She reached up to kiss him on the lips, even though they were out on the street where a few other people could see as they strolled by.

He cleared his throat and looked around. As he looked in the direction of the blacksmith shop, he turned around. "Why don't you go on in the carriage and rest? I need to talk to Sam for a moment about one of Midnight's shoes."

She agreed, as she began to feel nauseous once again and stumbled her way in.

"Are you all right, dear?" he asked anxiously.

"Yes, I'm fine. Just lost my footing a little."

She sat down as he closed the door and walked in the direction of the blacksmith shop. She closed her eyes and willed the nausea to go away, thinking perhaps it was only that she was hungry and thirsty and cold. Yes, that must be it. Or the germ.

Two

William walked away from the carriage realizing that Ginny had gone pale, and that he had seen her retching earlier that morning. He wondered if she could be with child. Excitement began to stir inside of him. A child with Ginny would be wonderful. He had lost a child as well as his first wife back when he was in the war many years ago, and even though Ginny insisted she didn't want a child yet, didn't want to share him yet as they had only been married for six months, he suspected that she was most likely carrying one.

He was actually surprised she had not conceived before now. They had spent the whole summer in each other's arms, totally inseparable. He knew being married to her and being intimate with her would be wonderful, but it had surpassed his imaginings. *She* had surpassed his imaginings. She was a great lover, a quick learner. Their first time away from each other when she went to the academy and he to

Dr. Harrison, he had to admit was very hard for him. Ginny herself came home that day in tears; she'd missed him so much. They more than made up for it. And then after he helped her with her school work, they had another anatomy lesson long into the night.

They had gotten a little more used to being separated by now, but his heart still tugged at the sight of her after a long day apart. Even more so at the thought that she might be carrying his child. He feared he was becoming too dependent on her. He had never been so happy, and that scared him. He perhaps still feared losing her.

"William, what brings you here?" Sam said, disrupting his thoughts.

"Good evening, Sam. I was wondering if I might bring my horse by to-morrow morning for you to have a look at his right hind leg shoe. It seems to be bothering him, but I can't find the reason for it."

"Sure, I'd be happy to."

Sam had been extremely cooperative with William since their fight in May, ending with Sam being escorted off the plantation and later spending a couple of months in jail. William had actually helped Sam's mother move out of the boarding house and into the living areas above the shop while he was in jail. He'd felt sorry for the two of them, Sam having to become a man early in his life since his father died in the war, and Adaline being a widow with a high-spirited son. William also helped convince Mr. Holmes to re-hire Sam after he was released from jail, thinking that if he helped the young man out, he wouldn't cause further trouble for him or Ginny.

"Very well, then," William said. "I'll see you in the morning. Good evening. Tell your mother hello for me." He turned to go back to the carriage.

"Of course," he heard Sam say.

Once William reached the carriage, he opened the door and found Ginny asleep, nestled in her new coat, her blonde curls spilling out over the top. She was such a dear precious sweet thing, even more so when she was sleeping. She didn't even stir when he kissed her on the cheek, closed the door back gently, and slid into the front seat, prompting the horses down the road.

They reached their little cottage in a short time, and he gently woke her and helped her into the house.

"Oh!" she said when he first awoke her. "I'm sorry, William. I dozed off."

"You've had a long day; it's no wonder you fell asleep. Come on inside and let's see if Aunt Patsy has anything for us to eat."

His aunt had insisted that she cook two meals a day for the two of them, once in the morning to break their fast, and then in the evening when they came home from work and school. William had offered to hire a cook to come in at least for the evening meal, but his aunt insisted it would be her pleasure to cook for them. In exchange, he bought the food from the market and helped her with things around the house and garden when he had the time.

They walked inside the main house together and heard voices in the dining room. Judy, William's cousin, peeked her head around the corner after William shut the front door. "William! Ginny!"

"Judy! You're here early," William observed. She was carrying her own child, which he had confirmed back in the spring when he had brought Ginny and her family and friends to the house for a nice meal after a long day of shopping. Judy was married to a Northerner, Benjamin

Morehouse, who was in the military and stationed at Fort Monroe in nearby Newport News.

"Judy, how good to see you," Ginny said. They all greeted one another with hugs.

"As you can see, I'm as big as a house. William, my doctor in Newport News told me I'm due any time now, not at Christmas."

"Ah, well, what's a couple of weeks?" William said, laughing lightly.

"It's a lot when you're carrying a big cannonball in your belly!" she said, laughing herself. She put her hand on the small of her back. "I'm ready for this thing to come out. Anyway, that's why I came early. I didn't want to have it in Newport News – my doctor is a little disappointed, I think. But I told him, I insist that my dear cousin and his sweet wife deliver my baby."

"Is Ben still gone with the unit?" William asked.

"Yes. He's supposed to return on Christmas Eve. Fingers crossed," Judy said.

By this time, Aunt Patsy had joined them in the hall. "Come on in the dining room before your supper gets cold," she urged them.

William helped Ginny out of her new cape, which he bragged about getting for her, and the two other ladies declared it was beautiful. Robert, Aunt Patsy's youngest son, nodded his head and smiled. He was rendered mute after a war injury when a bullet got lodged inside his head.

They all sat down at the dining room table and ate and talked of their day. William noted more than once that Ginny barely ate anything, drank a little tea, and looked as pale as alabaster. She certainly was acting like a new mother-to-be. She finally asked to be excused, and William took her back over to their cottage.

"Forgive me for leaving early, but I'm not feeling well. I think I'll just go on to bed. You can go back over and visit with them if you'd like. I won't mind," she said.

"Nonsense. I want to be with my wife. Come, I'll help you out of your clothes and make you a nice cup of ginger tea." He stepped behind her to start undressing her.

"William, dear, I'm sorry, but I just don't feel like being…amorous tonight."

"I understand. But you still need help with all these buttons in the back."

He began unbuttoning her dress. Once she was undressed, he opened the dresser drawer and pulled out her favorite conservative nightgown that she wore once a month when they couldn't be intimate, and helped her into bed, pulling the covers up to her chin. He then lit a fire in the fireplace and put the kettle on to boil for the tea. By the time he'd turned around to see if Ginny needed anything, she was nearly asleep. He walked around the bed and kissed her forehead.

"I'm sorry," she said groggily. "I don't think I can drink the tea. Too…sleepy…"

"Rest well, my love."

He took the kettle off, got undressed himself, and turned down the oil lamp. He then slipped under the covers, snuggled up next to her, and they both drifted off to sleep.

Three

The next morning, Ginny got up before William, felt nauseous, and went out to the garden to expel mostly liquid and a little solid food. Once her stomach settled, she went back inside and stoked the kitchen fire to make some tea. She checked in the bedchamber to see if William was still asleep. He was. She decided to let him sleep in. He'd been working long hard hours with Dr. Harrison, and every other Saturday, he also helped another doctor at the Eastern Lunatic Asylum to get a well-rounded education in all aspects of being a doctor, including the mental diseases. He didn't have to go there today.

She thought she would make him breakfast. It was Saturday, and typically, they stayed in the cottage on Saturday and Sunday mornings, making their own breakfast. Gingerbread sounded really good, since Sam had mentioned the night before that his mother had made some, and it was one of William's favorites. She probably couldn't eat much of it herself, but she'd make some for him and the rest of the family. She searched the cupboard for molasses but couldn't find any, so she decided to go next-door and see if Aunt Patsy had any. She went back to the bedchamber and fetched a long pink dressing gown, buttoned it in front, and placed her feet inside some Indian moccasins that William made for her. He'd learned how to make them during the war from his Cherokee friend. He said that the skill came in handy during the hard winters in the latter years of the war when their only pair of shoes was too worn to wear. She liked wearing the moccasins around the house, as they were very comfortable and warm.

She headed outside where the air was cold enough to see her breath, and she hurried across the English herb garden over to the back door of the main house. Judy opened the door for her. Judy's long curly red hair hung down over a green dressing gown, which brought out the color of her eyes.

"What are you doing up so early this morning?" Judy asked her. "Get inside where it's warm. I've got a fire going in the kitchen."

"I was wondering if your mother had some molasses. I wanted to make William some gingerbread."

"I think we do. Why not make it here? We can double the batch and that way we can all enjoy some."

"All right. Let's do that." She felt some relief that she wouldn't have to do all the work by herself.

Judy walked over to a tall silver jug and held it up. "I was having some coffee. You want some?"

"Sure, I'll try some. My stomach has been a little unsettled lately."

Judy took a coffee cup out of the corner cupboard and poured some of the dark liquid into it. "Is that why you looked pale last night?" She glanced up at Ginny. "And this morning?"

Ginny blushed a little but tried to hide it by looking out the back window. "I think it may be a germ." She looked back at Judy. "I'll not get too close to you. I don't want you to be sick."

Judy sat the coffee cup and saucer on a small table next to another cup that was half empty. She sat down and motioned for Ginny to do the same. "Have you thought about the possibility that you might be with child?"

Ginny opened her eyes wide, looked at Judy and then back down at her coffee cup. "I have thought of that, but I'm hoping against it." She couldn't admit it to herself yet, let alone to Judy or even William.

"Why is that? Don't you want children?"

"Of course, but I'm not ready yet. I'm not ready to be a mother, not ready to share William with anyone else, not ready to put aside my nursing. It's too soon."

"It's not so bad. Sure, it's uncomfortable, but I look forward to taking care of a little one."

"Even with Benjamin being gone so much?"

"Yes, especially then. The baby will be company for me. It gets awfully lonely when Ben is gone."

Ginny took a sip of the hot coffee. "I bet it would. I don't know how you do it. I'd be so miserable without William if I couldn't see him every day."

"You're lucky to have the privilege of seeing him every day. It is very hard, but the times when we are together make up for the times when we are apart. It's a sacrifice we have to make for each other."

"I admire you for that. How are you feeling today? Any pains?"

"My back aches and my ankles are swollen, but otherwise I feel good."

"I'm not ready for my body to change like that," Ginny admitted. "You look so pretty in your condition, but I fear William would find me hideous if I carried a baby inside me like that."

Judy laughed lightly. "It's not me that's so big; well, not all me. It's mostly the baby. I plan to do what I can to get back to pre-baby size when I am able to. I know, you lose some self-confidence when you look like this, but William loves you so, he won't mind it at all, I'm sure of it. You know he lost his little girl before. I'm sure he's looking forward to another child."

Ginny took another sip of coffee as Judy got up and got out the flour, salt, sugar, and molasses. Ginny stood up and started helping, getting out a big bowl to mix the ingredients in. "I know he'd be thrilled if I was to conceive, but honestly, I'm terrified. Of labor mostly. I've helped a lot of women through it, some good, some not so good, and I just don't think I can handle it."

Judy stopped mixing and turned towards Ginny. "But you've got a doctor for a husband, and you yourself have plenty of knowledge. I'm sure you'll get through it just fine."

"I wish I shared your confidence. Of course, I trust William completely and have full confidence in him, but not so in myself. What if I can't do it? Can't get the baby out? I'd hate for William to have to cut on me. Not that he wouldn't do it right, but I'd hate for him to have to look at an ugly scar for the rest of my life."

"At least it would be your husband who made the scar, for the sake of your baby. That wouldn't be such a horrible thing."

"I'm just not ready for the whole process."

"You have plenty of time to get used to the idea, if you have conceived. Give yourself some time." Judy went back to measuring out some sugar.

"Please don't tell William yet. I haven't talked with him about it. I'm just not ready," Ginny said.

"All right. It's just between us girls, then."

"Thank you. I'll go outside and get some butter and eggs."

As she walked into the hall, Robert walked towards her, nodded his morning greeting, and went into the kitchen to get his morning cup of coffee. Ginny went out the back door and over to the little milk house where they stored milk and butter and then to the hen house for some eggs and brought them back inside. Robert was not there, so she went back to helping Judy with the gingerbread. The two of them worked together, adding ingredients, stirring, and finally they put the batter in a long pan and placed it in the cooking shelf above the kitchen fire. They were in the process of cracking eggs open to fry when Ginny looked down at her left hand and realized that her ring was missing.

She gasped. "My wedding ring! It's gone!"

She reached inside the pockets of her dressing gown but didn't find it.

"Where do you think it could be?" Judy asked.

"I have no idea."

"Did you have it on last night at supper? Maybe it's in the dining room."

They both rushed over to search the dining room table, floor, and then all through the house, but didn't see it anywhere. Ginny began to get nauseous again, with worry this time.

"I'll go check the cottage and see if it's over there, or perhaps I dropped it in the milk house or chicken coop."

Before she made it into the hallway, however, William came in through the back door.

"There's my girl." He took Ginny in his arms and kissed her on the top of her head. "How are you feeling this morning?"

"I'm fine," she said, forcing a smile. She was still nauseous, even more so now, trying to hide from her husband the fact that she'd lost her wedding ring. She felt so careless, and now that he was awake, she would have to wait until later to search for it.

"You don't look fine. You're still pale. Why are you over here, anyway?" He looked over at Judy. "Good morning, Judy."

"Morning, William," she said, smiling.

"I wanted to make you some gingerbread, but we were out of molasses," Ginny said. "Judy suggested that I stay here and make enough for everyone, so that's what we've been doing. I wanted to let you sleep since you don't have to go to the asylum today."

"Aren't you so sweet?" He hugged her a long moment in front of Judy, but Ginny wasn't embarrassed. Her thoughts drifted back and forth between the possibility that she was carrying his child and wondering where her wedding ring could be, but she didn't say a word about either at this time.

Four

A week later, Ginny still had not found her wedding ring. She'd searched the cottage from top to bottom. Searched the stables, the yard, the herb garden, the hen house, the milk house, everywhere she could think of. She'd reached the conclusion that she had lost it the night that William gave her the new coat. Near the blacksmith shop. Near Sam. She was convinced that he had found it, knowing it was hers, and was keeping it or had already sold it. He was just spiteful enough to do something like that.

She thought about asking Robert if he had seen it, but she was sure it happened when she was at Sam's, not at the house.

It was a quiet Thursday evening, and she and William had just come back to the cottage after a nice supper of stew over at Aunt Patsy's. Judy had still not delivered her baby and seemed to grow larger every day. Ginny was sitting in their little parlor studying anatomy charts when William brought her a cup of ginger tea. She noticed he had been doing that every day for the past week, after supper. She wondered if he suspected her condition.

She was still heaving after each meal, so she most likely did not have a germ but was carrying a child. When she arose in the morning, it would take a couple of hours for her stomach to settle before she could go to class. Therefore, she had to rise early and go to bed early. She and William had also not been intimate. She was fearful she would get nauseous in the middle of it and retch all over him. That would be disastrous.

"Can we talk about something?" William asked her as he sat down across from her in a pale blue winged-back chair. The look on his face worried Ginny. She wondered if he wanted to talk about her possible confinement or the fact that she'd lost her wedding ring. She self-consciously hid her left hand under her dress.

"What about?" she asked, trying to be nonchalant, glancing up at him and then back down at her charts.

"About your paleness and heaving after meals lately. Are you feeling all right?"

Ginny looked up at his worried face. "It's just a germ," she said quickly. "I probably picked it up at the academy. That's why I haven't wanted to be…intimate lately. I'm sorry."

"Would a germ also cause you to miss a cycle?"

She gasped and widened her eyes in shock.

"I am your husband as well as a doctor. Did you think I wouldn't notice?"

She did not want to talk about this now, did not want to accept what he was insinuating. "Yes, as a matter of fact, a germ can cause a woman to be late with her cycle. You should know that."

He studied her eyes intently. "Are you sure that's all it is?"

"Yes, I'm sure."

"You don't want me to examine you?"

"No, that's not necessary."

He sighed, still looking into her eyes. "Very well. But if it doesn't get better in a week, you should let me do a thorough examination."

She nodded her head. "One week." She looked back down at her anatomy charts, trying to dismiss the conversation – and her nervousness.

They heard caroling outside, and William got up to look out the window. "Come look."

Ginny stood up and walked over beside him to look out. There were several men and women over in front of the white picket fence of the main house, singing Christmas carols. William and Ginny walked out the front door of the cottage so they could hear better. He put his arms around her, pulling her close.

"This is nice," Ginny said. She felt warm and content in his embrace, happier than she had been in a week, her nervousness dissipating. She leaned her head against his chest and up under his chin, and sighed. She'd been avoiding much physical contact with him lately, and now it seemed foolish. He seemed to know exactly what she needed right now. Comfort.

William was trying to do more for Ginny, in case she had conceived. The look on her face when he asked her about missing a cycle was one of shock. She was terrified of conceiving. She'd told him before that she hoped she didn't conceive anytime soon, that she didn't want to share him with anyone else yet. But he suspected there was more to it than that. She seemed literally frightened. Surely she knew enough about medicine and her own body to know she had to be carrying a child. He didn't think a germ would have lasted this long.

So, he would just continue to do things for her to make her more comfortable and avoid the subject. He'd massaged her neck, shoulders, and lower back each evening before they went to sleep. She'd been eating more and yet excusing herself after meals to take a walk in the garden – alone – stressing that she needed a little solitude to collect her thoughts for what she had to do for school. But he knew better. She was going out to heave. He had watched her that very evening and saw her go behind the stables. He followed her quietly, not letting her see him, and sure enough saw her throw up the meal she'd just eaten. And then she did something that broke his heart. She cried. He wanted to take her in his arms and tell her it was all right but didn't want to embarrass her. So he'd gone back inside to wait for her to come back in and then talk to her about it.

Yet she refused to admit it to him, and that made him sad. He'd just have to be patient and let her get used to the idea. He wanted her to be happy about having his child, not sad. It was perhaps just immaturity and uncertainty about being a mother and the changes in her body that upset her, and the uncomfortable sickness that went along with it.

"I will miss this kind of thing when we move back to Charles City County. There is always something going on here in Williamsburg," Ginny said to him, bringing his thoughts back to the present.

"Yes, that's true. But I intend to look into opening an office in the business area of Charles City County so that we could still enjoy a little city life during the week, and then retreat to our Forest home at week's end."

She looked up to face him. "That sounds wonderful." She started to kiss him but then looked away.

He turned her chin up so that he could kiss her, sweetly, softly.

"I don't want you to get my germ," she said, her eyes sorrowful. She was really putting up a convincing act with this germ excuse. Was she now afraid to kiss him? Afraid he would force her to have relations? Of course, he would not. She obviously did not feel amorous enough for intimacy, so he would be content to hold her in his arms, caress her, and massage her as much as she'd let him. That would have to do for now.

Five

On the last day of school until after the holidays, Ginny waited in front of the academy for William's carriage. Judy had still not had her baby, so it seemed that William had been correct about the baby's timing, after all. Ginny was getting nervous, however, as they were planning to go to Charles City County for Christmas. Christmas Eve was only five days away. If Judy didn't have her baby before then, they'd have to stay in the cottage for Christmas.

Ginny had hoped they could spend Christmas Eve in their new Forest home. Her mother said the first floor was completed and livable, although the upstairs rooms were not yet finished. They planned to sleep in one of the first floor rooms, the parlor or the library, and William had already ordered a couple of pieces of furniture and had them sent to the house. He promised she would love the things he'd picked out for their new home, and that she could pick out other things to add to it later. Perhaps next year, they'd be able to sleep upstairs in their bedchambers.

As Ginny was contemplating all of this, she saw Sam come walking up the road, heading towards the blacksmith shop. She ignored him until he got closer.

"Hello, Mrs. Brown," he said politely, tipping his hat. He was wearing a new suit complete with bowtie and top hat. It looked quite expensive for someone of his profession. She felt sure he had indeed kept her ring and sold it for quite a bit of money. William never did tell her how much he paid for it, but she was sure it was worth a lot.

She tried to remain cordial. "Afternoon, Mr. Bowen. Are you going someplace special?" She raised an eyebrow up in question.

"As a matter of fact, I am. I've a special party my mother and I are invited to, at Mr. Holmes' house. His wife's family is apparently fairly wealthy, and she recently inherited a big fine place over off of Henry Street near the graveyard."

"Oh. That sounds nice." She remained aloof and straight-faced.

"In case you're wondering, I borrowed this outfit. You know I cannot afford such nice attire."

"I was wondering, yes," she admitted. She still didn't believe him, as he was a habitual liar. "Enjoy your party, Mr. Bowen." She hoped he would move along and out of her sight.

"Thank you. You have yourself a nice evening, as well," he said, smiling. He walked away whistling a Christmas carol.

She rolled her eyes. She started looking for William again, who was late like he had been a fortnight ago. She was glad that at least this time she had a nice warm cape to keep her comfortable.

William soon arrived in a rush, worry on his face.

"What's wrong, William?" she asked, as he jumped out of the carriage quickly.

"It's Judy. She's gone into labor."

"Finally," she said.

He smiled as he took her books from her and put them inside the carriage, then turned to assist her inside.

It was then she realized that she really didn't want to be part of this labor, after all. She was dreadfully nervous. Not because it would be her first time assisting William in a delivery, but because this was the first delivery she would be helping with since she realized she herself was with child. She felt the urge to heave, just thinking about it.

William drove the horses back to his aunt's house, helped Ginny out of the carriage, and she helped him unhook the horses from the carriage. William put them in the stables and then they walked to the house together, arm in arm.

"Are you excited? This will be the first time we've worked together since Madeline lost her baby," William said.

"Yes, of course," she said, forcing a smile. Madeline Wellington was her step-father's sister, and also her Cousin Ethan's wife. Ginny had helped William when Madeline miscarried a baby last spring.

Once inside the house, they went upstairs to the room where Judy was staying.

"How far apart are your pains?" William asked her and his aunt, who was sitting in a chair by Judy's bed.

"Twenty minutes," Aunt Patsy said. "She's got a little ways to go yet."

"All right. Ginny, can you go boil some water and have some clean linens available?"

"Yes, of course."

"We'll need to have a place for the baby once he or she has arrived. Do you have clothing ready?"

"Yes," Judy answered. "Over there on the bassinette, along with a clean linen to wrap the baby in."

"Good."

Aunt Patsy had found Judy's old bassinette down in the storage area of the cellar, and had cleaned it all up for her new grandchild.

They spent the next hour getting hot water, clean linens, and Robert made a pot of strong coffee for William and Ginny, in case the laboring went into the wee hours of the morning, while Judy kept having pains far apart.

"Has your water broken yet?" William asked her.

"No," Judy answered.

The baby had apparently decided to take its time coming out. All four of them took turns sitting up with Judy and helping her get through the pains, while the other two rested, ate supper, and finally took turns sleeping. By three o'clock in the morning, Judy was exhausted, and William was the only one up with her.

"Judy, I don't think this baby is coming anytime soon. Why don't you try to get some sleep? I'll give you a shot of whiskey to help. Then in the morning, we can all start fresh and see if the baby is ready to come out then."

"All right. Whatever you think is the right thing to do, let's do it. I need some rest. I'm exhausted."

He left the room momentarily and came back with a small shot glass full of amber liquid, which he gave Judy to drink. She gulped it down with eyes closed and a pained look on her face. He took the glass from her, and she succumbed to sleep fairly quickly.

William checked on his aunt, who was asleep in her bedchamber and Robert in his, and then went next-door to the cottage where he had already sent Ginny to sleep hours ago. She had done her usual after-supper retching earlier, in secret, of course, and he told her to go on and get some sleep. She was too nauseated to be of much help.

He stripped his clothes off and crawled in, nestled against her warm body, and drifted off to sleep.

Six

The next morning, William awoke before dawn and started getting dressed to go help deliver Judy's baby. Ginny woke up while he was in the middle of dressing.

"William?"

"Hmm?" He glanced over at her and smiled.

"Has Judy had her baby yet?"

"No. I gave her some whiskey at about three in the morning and told her to get some sleep."

"Oh." Ginny rubbed her eyes. "Good, I didn't miss anything."

"You don't have to do anything if you don't want to. I know how tired you are," William said, walking around to sit on the bed beside her.

She sat up and reached for him. He took her sleepy body in his arms, and she laid her head against his chest. Finally she said, "No, I want to help you. You do need me. Just give me a few minutes to wake up."

She let go and looked up at him, and he kissed her softly on the lips. He pushed her disheveled hair away from her face and smiled. Her natural beauty still took his breath away, even in the first light of morning. "Take all the time you need. I'll appreciate your help, but only if you feel like it."

He then left her and went over to the main house where Aunt Patsy had already made some strong coffee, and she handed him a cup.

"How's Judy this morning?" he asked.

"Still sleeping."

"We'll let her be for the moment. Have you started some water boiling yet?"

"Got it started. I'm going to fix you some eggs before you get down to work."

"Sounds good."

Robert came in and patted William on the shoulder, smiled, and got his own cup of coffee.

William walked upstairs to check on Judy, who was indeed still sleeping. He hoped everything went smoothly today. He knew he could send for Dr. Harrison if something went wrong, but he wanted to be able to do this on his own…and with Ginny, if she felt up to it. She had helped deliver babies in the past, so she should be well-equipped for the job.

He walked back downstairs and found Ginny talking with his aunt.

"That was fast," he said.

She smiled and then sipped her own cup of coffee.

"Let's take these eggs into the dining room before they get cold," his aunt said. "They're hot and ready. Should we take some up to Judy? I hate for her to go hungry."

"It's probably not a good thing for her to eat, as it may interfere with delivery. If her body is busy digesting food, it may not get all the things it needs to push the baby out. She'll need energy, though. She could have some tea with honey."

"I'll go make some right now, then," Aunt Patsy said.

Later that morning, Judy was in the middle of more pains, but still no baby to be seen yet. William got her up and walked her through the house a couple of times after she awoke, trying to get gravity to pull the baby down, but the pains were still fifteen minutes apart. William let her have little sips of tea every now and then so she wouldn't get dehydrated.

"William! You have to do something to make this baby come out. I can't take much more of this," Judy said later that afternoon, pulling her sweaty red hair away from her face.

"Judy, I wish I knew what to do. It won't come out until it's ready to."

That's when her water finally broke. "I feel something coming out. I think my water broke," she said, smiling for the first time that day.

Ginny went to get the clean linens and boiling water, and brought a big pitcher of it upstairs. She had had a harder time hiding her bouts of emesis while being around William and his aunt all day, but she kept trying to hide it. She was starting to get nervous about Judy's delivery. It made her think about her own delivery in eight or nine months.

When she reached the bedchamber again, Judy was having pains that were a lot stronger and closer together. She went to her side and held her hand through the pains, talking to her about Newport News and her new neighbors where she was living now, to distract her.

Judy complained of back pain in addition to the abdominal pains, and Ginny got her to lean forward so she could massage her lower back during some of the pains.

When Judy got a really intense pain, worse than all the others, she cried out. "Oh, God! William, do something. I'm so weak. I can't take this."

"Ginny, would you get her some laudanum, please. It's over there on the table," William said.

Ginny couldn't move. She was suddenly overcome with fear and couldn't even comprehend what William had just asked her to do.

"Ginny?" William said again. "Did you hear me?"

She kept looking at the awful expression on Judy's face, thinking about herself going through that same pain. She didn't want to go through that.

"Ginny!" William called to her sternly. She looked over at him slowly, in a daze.

"Huh?" She blinked, and he walked around the bed and took her by the arms.

"Why don't you take a break for a moment out in the hall or go outside and get some air."

She was vaguely aware of him helping her out the door and placing her on a fainting couch out in the hall.

"Sit here and collect yourself a minute. I'll be right back."

He left her for a moment with the door open, and she watched him get a bottle off of the little side table and poured some in a glass and gave it to Judy. He had given her medicine. Laudanum. That's what he'd asked her to do. She felt foggy in the head like she was the one who'd taken laudanum.

Once Judy took that and settled back on the bed, William came back out and sat beside Ginny.

"I'm sorry. You told me to give her laudanum, didn't you?"

"Are you all right?" He put his arms around her and pulled her against his chest.

She felt herself start to weep. "No, I'm not."

He rubbed her face gently and kissed the top of her head.

"I don't want to go through that."

"It'll be all right," was all that he said.

Two hours later, it was time for Judy to start pushing the baby out. William was ready.

"I've got to push now. Please, I have to," Judy wailed.

Ginny had come back into the room and was doing better at soothing Judy and distracting her, and rubbing her back for her through the pains. Her earlier look of panic had changed to indifference, like she was distancing herself from what was happening. At least she was helping Judy, which was helping him.

"Yes, you can push now. Every time the urge comes, push with everything you've got. Are you ready?"

Judy nodded, took a deep breath, and started pushing, her face turning red. She grunted and wailed as she pushed, and William stood by at the end to wait for the baby to come out. He could see the head.

"I see the head now, Judy."

One more grunt, and then Judy collapsed back to rest, the urge gone. Ginny, who had been holding her hand, let go of it and walked around beside William. He showed her the baby's head. He looked at her, and she had that look of panic again. She clutched at her throat and stomach, and he could see perspiration develop on her cheeks and upper lip.

"Ginny? Stay with me."

"I've got to go…" Ginny said, running out the door.

"I'll be right back, Judy. Aunt Patsy, stay right here in case she has another urge to push."

Patsy nodded and took William's place while he went out to check on Ginny, and Robert got up from the corner chair to hold Judy's hand.

William found Ginny on the fainting couch out in the hall again.

"Ginny, are you all right?" He stood in front of her.

"How…how can such a big baby come through such a tiny space?" She was lost in worries and fears of childbirth.

"Ginny, why don't you go back to the cottage and rest?"

"No," she said adamantly. "I want to help, but…"

"Then I need you to help keep her calm. I can't have you heaving or being nervous in there. It's not good for her delivery. If you want to help, come back when you have calmed down."

He kissed her head, as she was leaning over looking at the floor, and went back to help Judy.

He'd missed another push, and the baby's head was out, facedown and held by Patsy. William took over holding the head before the next push, at which time Ginny came back in and held Judy's other hand again. She looked more reserved and confident. After one more push, William could tell the sex of the baby.

"You've got a little girl, Judy."

She pushed one more time, and the little girl came out. Ginny was ready with a cloth to clean the baby off. William handed the baby to Ginny, who held her while he examined her.

"She has all of her fingers and toes," he said.

Judy smiled. "Let me hold her," she said.

Ginny wrapped her in a clean blanket and placed her in Judy's arms.

"You're perfect," Judy said to the baby.

William had tears in his eyes, and he felt a hand on top of his. Ginny's. He squeezed it tightly.

"What are you going to name her?" Ginny asked.

"Minnie, after her grandmother. It's also a variation of Benjamin. Just wait until your father sees you," she said to the baby.

Minnie cried out for the first time, just once, seemingly in answer.

"I agree," Judy said. "That was a lot of work, wasn't it?" She kissed Minnie's cheek and held her close. "But well worth it."

Seven

Just before sunset, after cleaning up, William went outside and found Ginny in the garden under the trellis, retching. When she was all done, she wiped her mouth with the back of her hand and sat down on the bench and started crying, covering her face up with her hands. He couldn't stand it anymore. He went to her this time.

"Ginny," he called as he walked towards her.

She looked up with a panicked, embarrassed look on her face.

"Sweetheart, please don't cry. You're breaking my heart."

He sat down beside her and took her in his arms. She squeezed him tightly and cried loudly into his overcoat.

"I'm so sorry, William. I messed up. I've never done that before with Fanny, I swear it. You must think me silly and immature."

Fanny was an ex-slave that had lived on the same

plantation as Ginny when they were courting, and Ginny used to help her deliver babies.

"Nonsense. It affected you more this time. Do you know why?"

She raised up to look him in the eyes. "Yes, I think so."

"Do you want to talk about it?" He wiped the tears out from under her eyes with his thumb.

She looked down at his chest. When she didn't answer, he continued. "It's been a week, and you're still having emesis. You promised me you would let me examine you."

She looked back up at his face with a frightened look. He loathed seeing her look at him that way. It was obviously still too painful for her to talk about. Perhaps she just needed more time with Minnie, see how precious a baby can be, to make her desire to have one of her own. He would just continue to soothe her as best he could.

"If you need more time, that's fine. But would you do me a favor?"

"What is it?" She sniffed loudly.

"Can we put off going to Charles City another day or two, so we can help Judy get used to being a mama. She'll need a lot of rest, especially for the next twenty-four hours, until Benjamin can get here. Would you help her with the baby while she naps some?"

"Yes, of course." She smiled and took a deep breath and sighed shakily.

"Thank you." He took her back in his arms again, and she clutched her arms around his back. "You've been through a lot today, why don't I draw you a bath?"

She nodded her head. "That sounds nice."

An hour later, Ginny was soaking in a tub of hot water out in the wash house, washing with some of the lilac goat's milk soap given to her by Madeline. William had done everything for her bath – heated the water, poured it all in the tub, got her pink dressing gown, her favorite soap, and a soft drying towel and set it all up for her in the wash house. All she'd had to do was show up. He was gentle and sweet. She'd never felt so pampered before.

He was being so nice that it made her feel guilty. She wished she could just be bold and talk to him about the possibility – the probability – that she was carrying his child, but she just couldn't yet. She didn't want him to know how nervous she was, didn't want him to think she wasn't happy about having his child…until she actually was happy about it.

She'd been so awful during Judy's delivery. She felt so inept, so childish. She ran out not once but twice. She was so afraid she would heave there in the bedchamber; she just had to get out. She felt like she had disappointed William, that she had let him down when he needed her, and she felt just awful about that. He didn't deserve to be treated that way, and yet he was being so gentle, so caring.

She had to do something for him, so she would help Judy out by watching little Minnie for her while she napped and while Aunt Patsy cooked, as William had asked her to.

She finished her bath, covered up with the dressing gown, and then went over to the cottage to get dressed. Once she had on a comfortable grey cotton dress, she walked over to the main house and upstairs to see Judy, who was feeding Minnie.

"Judy, how are you feeling?"

"Tired," she said, smiling, "but happy. Happy it's over with, and happy to have this precious little bundle of joy."

She looked down at the baby. "Isn't she beautiful?"

Ginny looked at the baby as she continued suckling milk from her mother. "Yes," Ginny said, smiling.

Minnie stopped nursing, apparently satiated, and Judy wrapped her up in a blanket and fixed her own clothing.

"Shall I take her for you? You can take a nap before supper."

"That sounds wonderful." She took a drink of water from a nearby glass. "Thank you Ginny."

Ginny reached down and picked up Minnie and held her close. It was the first time she'd looked at her without all the blood, without the crying, and she truly was beautiful. "You're right. She is beautiful," she said. When she looked at Judy for a response, she saw that she had already fallen asleep.

Ginny took the baby out of the bedchamber and sat on the fainting couch out in the hall so she would be close. Aunt Patsy was down in the kitchen preparing something to eat, and William was resting in the parlor. Ginny held Minnie and watched her. She looked up at Ginny with big blue eyes.

"Hey, sweetie. Aren't you a pretty thing?"

She looked down as the baby wiggled an arm outside of the blanket. Before Ginny replaced the blanket back around her, she looked at Minnie's tiny hand and fingers. She took her little hand in her big one, and Minnie surprised her by squeezing one of her fingers.

"What a firm grip you have," she said, half laughing. "Such tiny delicate fingers and fingernails. You really are precious."

The baby let go of her finger and yawned.

"What a sweet yawn. You want to sleep, sweetie?"

She wrapped the baby's arm back inside the blanket and

leaned back in the fainting couch and rocked her gently. As she hummed "Silent Night," she smiled, watching the baby's eyes droop and finally close, and she fell asleep in Ginny's arms.

"So precious," she whispered.

William watched Ginny over the next two days as she grew more comfortable with being around the baby, volunteering to hold her, walk her around the house, and sing to her. She also seemed to have grown more comfortable with her own condition. He didn't see her crying again and when he observed her coming back inside from retching, she smiled at him instead of looking sad. It made his heart glad. He hoped that she was seeing past the delivery to the miracle of a baby.

The night before they were to go to Charles City County, she was getting undressed while he watched her from the bed. She had just come back to the cottage from helping Judy get Minnie to sleep.

"Did you get Minnie put to bed?"

"Yes. She's in her bassinette beside her mother, both asleep. I'm going to miss both of them."

He smiled at her and held the blankets out for her. She joined him on the bed, crawling under the covers and cuddling up next to him.

"Have you heaved for the last time this evening?"

She looked up at him sharply. Then she half-smiled. "Yes. William, I have a confession to make. One I think you already know about."

"Yes?" He held his breath. He'd been waiting for this conversation for a fortnight.

"I think I am with child. You may examine me if you like, but I am fairly certain that this is the reason for all the heaving."

He smiled at her tentatively. "And are you happy about this?"

"I was not at first, but I am beginning to."

He nearly crushed her in a tight embrace. "That makes me so happy."

She laughed lightly. "I take it you are glad to have a baby?"

"Ecstatic." He pushed a wisp of her hair behind her ear and kissed her neck. He felt her shiver. "What a wonderful Christmas present."

She smiled. "Yes, it is."

He kissed her tenderly.

"How long have you known?" she asked.

"I have suspected it since the night I gave you the cape."

"That is the same day I suspected it, as well. I'm sorry, William. I was scared, you see? I'm still scared, but…" She took a deep breath and sighed. "I can see the good in the end, how precious and sweet a baby can be. I can actually say now that by the time it is my turn to go through all of that laboring, I will be ready. I think."

"I know you're frightened, but I'll be with you." He caressed her arm up and down slowly.

"That's all I want. I don't want to go through any of that without you. Do you promise you won't leave me, like Benjamin?"

"I promise I'll be with you. Nothing could keep me away. I'll be with you every step of the way. I have more knowledge this time around, with this baby. I'll do everything in my power to keep both of you safe and well."

She caressed his cheek. "Are you still worried about losing us, like you did Rachel and Emily?"

He nodded. "Yes, sometimes." He had lost his first wife and child to consumption.

She kissed him deeply, deeper than she had in quite a while.

"You may examine me now, if you'd like."

"Mmm, yes, I would like…"

Eight

The next morning, William and Ginny packed two trunks of clothes and necessities along with baskets of food to put in the carriage for their journey to Charles City County where their new home and Ginny's family awaited.

William had examined her the night before…in more ways than one. She was indeed carrying his child, and based on the date of her last cycle and her symptoms, he expected her to deliver in August. They celebrated by having relations, gently, slowly.

He had been concerned about her physical symptoms. "Are you sure you feel like being intimate?"

"Yes. I'm sorry I haven't wanted to in a while. I didn't want to be sick on you." He laughed lightly. "I'm fine right now, I promise. Please, I need you."

"Oh, Ginny…"

Now they were saying good-bye to Aunt Patsy, Robert, Judy, and little Minnie, promising they would return in a fortnight.

The journey took a couple of hours. Ginny sat inside the carriage while William drove their horses out front. He drove at a slow pace, in his words, so as not to induce nausea for her. She had plenty of time to ponder about her condition, their future baby. She was actually now looking forward to having a baby. She wondered if it would be a boy or a girl. What would they name it? Who would it look like? She looked forward to nursing and caring for it, this tiny being that would be woven together from a part of her and a part of William, because of their love for each other. She rubbed the lower part of her abdomen, wondering about all these things.

She also wondered and worried about what happened to her ring. She had asked Robert using hand motions, but he shook his head that he had not seen it. She tried to convey to him to swear to secrecy so he wouldn't tell William, to which he agreed. She still suspected that Sam had stolen it and then sold it, and if he did, she might have to shoot him. After William had been so nice to him, it would be foolish of him to do something like that. He could be jobless and out on the streets in a heartbeat if he wasn't careful.

If Sam had not taken the ring, then she had no idea what could have happened to it, and once again she dreaded having to tell William about it. She could just imagine how disappointed he would be, and it would break her heart to disappoint him…again.

They arrived at Magnolia Grove Plantation to be greeted first by Sambo and Lidia, both ex-slaves, who were recently wed at the plantation, and then by Ginny's mother,

Catherine, her husband Jonas, and Ginny's half-siblings, Jonathon and Emma. William helped Ginny into the house where she sat in the parlor with her mother and the little ones while he and Jonas moved their trunks into Ginny's old room on the second floor temporarily. The plan was to spend the first night with her family, and then the next day, they would go to their partially refurbished home in the woods and spend the night for Christmas Eve and come back on Christmas Day.

Lidia served the ladies tea and cinnamon scones in the parlor. Ginny told her mother of her confinement, and her reaction was joyous. She gasped and stood up quickly to hug her.

"Oh, Ginny. I'm so happy for you." She held her at arm's length. "How are you feeling?"

"Sick. A lot." She smiled briefly. "It takes me a while to get the nausea to go away in the mornings after I have coffee and a little breakfast."

"Well, as I'm sure you know, that will most likely only last about three months. Then you'll feel a whole lot better."

"I look forward to that," Ginny said. "We helped Judy deliver her baby – it was a little girl."

"Oh, that's wonderful. What did she name it?"

"Minnie, after Judy's husband's mother."

"How did the delivery go?"

"It took a really long time, and that made me extremely nervous," she admitted. "William helped me to get past my nervousness so that we could help Judy with her own anxieties and she could get Minnie out."

"It is good that you have William to help you through all of this."

"Yes, it is. He's been really patient with me, and he's so happy to have another baby."

"I'm so glad for you both."

"What is that beautiful red flower over there? Those leaves are huge," Ginny said, pointing to a potted plant sitting on the floor on one side of the fireplace.

"That's a poinsettia. Do you like it?"

"Yes, very much."

"They were selling them in the market. Supposedly, they came from down South somewhere, originating in Mexico, I believe."

"How interesting. I'm surprised they will live up here, as cold as it is right now."

"That's why I placed it near the fire, so it will stay warm. Madeline and I got one for you and William, too. You'll see it in your new home."

"You did? Oh, thank you, Mother." She hugged her excitedly.

William and Jonas joined them in the parlor then. They all chatted a while, had a nice big meal in the dining room, prepared by Lidia, and then Ginny went upstairs to her old room to rest.

She had every intention of taking a nap, but she started thinking about spending Christmas in their new home and exchanging gifts, and she knew the happy spirits of the season would be dampened by the fact that she didn't have her wedding ring. She would have to tell him.

"Ginny? What's wrong?" William's voice startled her. She hadn't heard him come into the room. He closed the door quietly, and she quickly straightened up and tried to hide her tears.

"Is something bothering you? Do you feel bad?" he asked.

She wiped her eyes with her handkerchief and blew her nose. She couldn't tell him the reason for her tears yet. They had plenty of time to discuss that in the next two days.

"No, I'm just tired from the trip. I cry easily these days, it seems. Forgive me."

She smiled, and he sat down beside her on the bed and took her in his arms.

"I understand," he said.

They spent the rest of the evening in the company of family and retired early.

In the morning, the family enjoyed a big hot breakfast in the dining room, and then William and Ginny's carriage was packed up once again for their journey into the woods to their house. Jonas was going to drive the carriage over and drop Ginny and William off at the house, unloading the trunks and some food. They couldn't drive themselves over because there was no stable for the horses to stay in. It was getting much too cold to leave them outside without a shelter.

Ginny lay against William's chest inside the carriage for the short ride, and they looked out the windows and talked about the landscape. The last time they had come to these woods had been at the end of the summer, and everything had been green and thick. Now, only pine, magnolia, and a few cedar trees kept their green leaves. Patches of snow dotted the forest floor here and there from a previous snow.

Once they reached the long carriageway to their Forest Plantation house, Ginny had tears at her first look. The whole outside of the house was complete again, with a roof on top where there hadn't been before, and four tall chimneys. All of the windows were perfect again, hurricane shutters hanging in place. In front of the house was a circular drive for the carriages, which encircled a small garden area that had been cleared of weeds to reveal dormant azalea bushes and dark green boxwood.

They disembarked the carriage, and Jonas and William lifted the trunks off and took them inside the house while Ginny picked up one of the baskets of food. Before they opened the front door, which was adorned with an evergreen wreath made of Leyland cypress, magnolia boughs, and brightened up with holly berries and a red velvet bow, Jonas stopped them.

"Before you go inside, I wanted you to know that the ladies have gotten together and decorated the house for you – just this floor, the finished parts. Your mother," he said to Ginny, "and Madeline have been over here every day after school working hard so you would have a nice place to spend your first Christmas together in. It's their Christmas presents to you both." He paused and cleared his throat. "And one big gift is from me. You'll know what it is when you see it, in the parlor. It was no longer needed at our house, and I felt you should have it. I had originally bought it for you, after all."

Ginny was giddy with excitement to see what they had done and marveled at the mystery of what Jonas had given her. He slowly opened the door and let Ginny go inside first. Her jaw dropped at the wonder of what she saw. The wide hallway had new gleaming dark wooden floors, and the staircase to the right of the front door was repaired, the bannister dressed with greenery swags and red velvet bows like on the front door.

To the left of the doorway was the dining room, and Ginny stepped inside to take it all in. There was a round table covered with a rich, deep red velvet covering, topped with a centerpiece of deep red camellias with yellow centers, glossy magnolia leaves, big pine cones, and quail feathers sticking out of a big white bowl. There were two place settings with white plates topped with white cloths decorated with holly berries and greenery and tied with tartan silky ribbons of red and green. Silverware lined up beside the plates, along with tall etched wine glasses, and slender long cream-hued candles atop crystal candle holders waited to be lit. A big metal bowl was filled with big red apples and pecans ready to be cracked open.

Two chairs that Ginny recognized as being from her mother's house rested in front of the table, each one adorned with juniper boughs and more camellias, holly berries, and tartan ribbon at the back.

Behind the glorious table was a brick fireplace with a white mantle that was draped with a cedar garland, big pinecones, more holly berries, a big green silky bow, and an ornate bowl filled with more camellias in red and pink, holly berries, and white mistletoe berries. Beside the fireplace was an ornate black metal rack filled with a tall stack of wood.

Ginny wandered back out into the hall as Jonas and William finished carrying in the trunks and baskets of food.

"I'll leave you two alone," Jonas said. "Merry Christmas." He kissed Ginny's cheek. "We'll see you tomorrow. Your mother wants me to come back and get you right at high noon. She has worked all week to prepare a special Christmas meal along with Lidia, so be ready for me when I come," he said, winking at William.

"All right," Ginny said, laughing. "We'll be ready. Merry Christmas."

"William." He tipped his hat.

"Merry Christmas, and thank you for everything."

Jonas left and William took Ginny in his arms.

"It's so beautiful, William! I can't believe how wonderful it looks in here. I remember when I could look up and see the blue sky." She laughed, and he kissed her nose lightly, which tickled and made her laugh more. "Now there's a beautiful ceiling." They both looked up. "And remember that raccoon? I hope he found a new home."

"Me, too. Come, let's have a look at our library."

She followed him excitedly, holding his hand, into the room where they had first professed their love for each other, and where William had given her…her wedding ring that she no longer had. She began to feel sad again.

Until she saw the room. There was a big mahogany desk facing away from the windows with a nice big leather chair behind it. An oil lamp sat on top of the desk along with an ink well and parchment paper. The mahogany fireplace had been refinished with an ornate leaf design across the front, and the big red poinsettia that her mother told her about had been placed on the floor near the fireplace. On either side of the fireplace were built-in bookshelves with a few books lining the shelves and a couple of gilded wooden frames with carved flowers waited to be filled with photographs or silhouettes. A sofa sat against the wall just the way she and William had pictured it last spring, in the same spot they had shared picnics and kisses. It had a curved back and was covered in a muted olive green, light red and beige pattern. Similarly colored pillows sat in the corners, embroidered with animals and flowers.

"Oh, William. It's beautiful. Just like we pictured it. The only thing missing are two chairs beside the fire."

"Do you really like it? I picked these two items out and had them delivered. I'll let you choose the chairs."

"That'll be exciting, decorating our new home." She looked into his eyes. "This is more than I imagined we would have in the house by now."

"Yes, and we've only seen half of it."

"We are going to be so happy here in this house." She cradled his cheeks with her hands, caressed his long sideburns, and pulled him down to kiss his lips. His arms went around her.

"Yes, it will be wonderful to have our own home. A place to live and love and raise our children." He placed his hand lovingly against her belly where the baby lay beneath.

Her heart started pounding with desire for him. It had been too long since they'd come together. Yes, they did so the night she confessed that she was with child, but it had been reserved, cautious. She wanted to let go of herself and all the feelings she'd been keeping inside, and show him the true depth of her ardor for him and the joy of having his child, the joy of being able to live in this house with him for many years to come.

She started taking her clothes off, beginning with her wool cape.

"Are you cold? I can light a fire."

She shook her head. "I can think of other ways to warm up." She began unbuttoning her dress in the back.

"What are you doing?" His eyes were shiny and bright with anticipation.

"What does it look like I'm doing?" She smiled seductively.

"Here? I know a much better place. Come with me."

She stopped him, putting her hand on his arm. "No, please. Love me now. Right here. In the room where our love began."

"Oh, Ginny…" He cupped her cheeks and kissed her fervently and then took his own overcoat off.

"I want to love you and show you how glad I am to be carrying our child…who was made just like this, from our loving each other."

"Ginny, I love you so."

They continued shedding their clothes in between kisses and loved each other desperately, wildly, not holding back, mouths seeking, tongues exploring, hands caressing. They moved over to the sofa to complete their act of love, panting, sweating, and calling each other's names in the throes of passion.

They collapsed together satiated and deliriously happy when it was over, smiling and collecting their breaths.

"I'd say we christened this new sofa pretty well," Ginny said, causing William to laugh loudly.

"Indeed we did."

He carefully rolled off of her onto the cold wooden floor. "Next time…the bed."

"We have a bed?"

"Of course, we do. Did you think we were going to camp out in here in the floor like we did last spring?"

"The thought did enter my mind," she smiled at the memories, at a time when they were courting and burning desperately for each other but held back until their wedding day.

"Let's go see the rest of the house."

She jumped up, and the two of them ran naked through the house, laughing and holding hands.

Nine

Across the hall from the library was the parlor. William held Ginny's hand and pulled her excitedly towards the room. There was a mistletoe ball hanging just above the threshold of the room, and they paused to kiss momentarily before entering the room. In this room was furniture from the bachelor's quarters at Magnolia Grove, including the burgundy settee, the burgundy and beige striped chair, and the armchair with ottoman in shades of brown and tan that used to be in William's room.

A small evergreen had been chopped to make a petite Christmas tree, which sat on a side table that was covered with fabric of muted reds and greens. On the tree were holly berries, white mistletoe berries, small pinecones, tartan bows, and little shiny thimbles.

An old trunk was used as a table in front of the settee where a silver tray held a gold-trimmed white teapot, teacups, and saucers on top of a tartan linen cloth with holly berries and a pine bough on the side of the tray. Another side table – again from William's bachelor room – sat beside the settee, which held a tall amber glass oil lamp and a couple of books, *A Christmas Carol* by Charles Dickens and a book of poems by William Wordsworth.

"This furniture looks familiar," Ginny remarked.

"Mhmm. Your mother volunteered the furniture, and I accepted but under the condition that it would be returned when we could afford to buy our own."

"That was nice. Oh, a piano! My piano!" The piano that she played at Magnolia Grove sat against the wall by the door. "Jonas's gift. That is so sweet. We shall sing Christmas carols later. Did you bring your harmonica?"

"Yes, of course."

She took his hand again. "We'll have to christen this room…later. Where's our new bed?"

He laughed and led her behind the parlor to a hidden room that could only be reached by going through the parlor. It was to the right of the parlor as you stepped inside from the hall, and tucked up under the staircase. This was where their temporary bedchamber would be. In the middle of the room was a high bed made of dark cherry wood, which William had ordered and arranged to be delivered to the house. Hopefully it wouldn't be too difficult to take it back apart and carry upstairs once that floor was completed.

Catherine and Madeline had decorated the bed with crisp white sheets, white lacy pillow cases, and a deep green covering that was reversible. A section of it was turned down away from the pillows to reveal a patchwork quilt of paisleys and flowers in different shades of green, blue, and white. The framework of the bed had a canopy over top, and long deep green velvet drapes hung, to be closed up at night for warmth.

"It's beautiful," Ginny said. Her jaw dropped in awe. "Where did this quilt come from? And these sheets?"

She quickly climbed the small steps up onto the high bed and slipped under the covers, running her fingers over the soft quilt.

He laughed at her pleasure and joined her under the covers.

"I let your mother pick that out. She and Madeline made this covering together."

"They did?"

He nodded. "Catherine told me."

"How sweet!"

There were small tables on both sides of the bed. On top of one was a green glass oil lamp and on the other was a pitcher for water, two glasses, and underneath in a hidden compartment was a chamber pot. The bed was between two windows and there were two more windows on either side of a fireplace on a side wall.

"I'll make us a fire," William said. He got up, put some logs in the fireplace, and lit a fire. When he heard snickering, he turned around and looked at Ginny. "What's so amusing?"

"Your white derriere sticking up while lighting that fire."

"Is that right? I'll have to punish you for that."

He came after her, climbing on the bed from the end, and she squealed, hiding herself under the covers.

He pulled the covers off really fast, and she squealed again. "I've got you now!" he said, and he began tickling her.

She laughed so hard, she almost sounded like she was crying.

"Stop, please! Mercy!" she said, between laughs, trying to catch her breath.

He stopped tickling and crawled under the covers, covering them both up. She took deep breaths and wiped happy tears from her eyes. He loved making her laugh. She'd not done enough of it for the past few weeks.

"I love you, Ginny," he said. "You make me feel young again, did you know that?" All of her exuberance, her vitality, was infectious.

She laughed again and snuggled against his chest. "I'm so glad." She laid one arm across his waist and caressed slowly with soft hands. Yawning, she said, "We shall try this bed out later. I need a nap first."

He chuckled. "Yes, you do. You've exerted yourself very well, I'd say."

He felt her smile. "Mhmm. Will you nap with me? You exerted yourself, as well."

"Yes, indeed."

They fell asleep in each other's arms contentedly.

When Ginny woke up, she was still in the same position as before, in William's arms. She moved her head slowly to look up and see if he was asleep. He tightened his arms around her, his eyes staring at her.

"You're awake?"

"Mhmm. I just woke up a short time ago. I've been watching you sleep, thinking about how much I love you. I'm so happy that you're having my baby, have I told you that?" He rubbed her arm with his thumb.

"Not today," she said, smiling. "I love you, too, my husband."

He kissed her, and she shifted so that she could reach him better.

"You're going to be a father again soon," she said between kisses. "What would you like this time, a boy or a girl?"

"Hmm, I really don't care, as long as it's healthy and beautiful like you." He moved a stray golden strand of her hair behind her ear.

She smiled. "What could we name a boy?" She played with a patch of hair in the middle of his chest. "I was thinking about Liam."

He kissed her nose. "Liam?"

She nodded. "Yes, Aunt Patsy told me that your father used to call you that when you were really young."

"She told you that?" he asked, surprised. "I had forgotten. I don't remember him calling me that, but my mother told me he did. You talked to Aunt Patsy about baby names?"

"Yes, well…I was just trying to get used to the idea, thinking of names."

"You talked to my aunt about your condition before you did with me?"

"Yes, and also Judy."

"What?" He pouted.

She laughed. "Yes, well sometimes it's nice to hear advice from another woman, someone who has actually had these symptoms before. No offense, Dr. Brown."

He smiled then. "None taken. So, Liam. That's another nickname you could have given me. You didn't want to call me Liam?"

"No. I like the name, but I think it would be nice to pass down your name without having two Williams in the same house. This way, we wouldn't get confused."

"I see," he said, smiling. "You never did give me a nickname, like you mused about when we were courting."

She laughed. "I was trying to take my mind off the fact that I wanted to ravage you, but you wouldn't let me."

"Ah, a distraction. I understand now."

"I call you husband," she said, more serious. "I'm the only one who can call you that."

"My sweet bride…" He kissed her, deep and long.

She heard a gurgle and realized it was her stomach.

"You're not going to be sick, are you?" William looked at her worriedly.

"No, actually…" she smiled. "I'm rather hungry."

"In that case, let me gather some food and we'll have a bed picnic." He got out from under the covers. "Don't laugh at my derriere again," he warned her. He put more logs on the fire and stoked it until the flames were high. Before leaving the room, he reached down, opened one of the trunks and pulled out a dressing gown, which he put on. Ginny laughed at him as he left the room.

She looked around and saw a hip bath in the corner with some bars of soap. That must be from Madeline, she thought, more of her goat's milk soap. She wondered what fragrance these were. She looked around thinking about what they could use this room for in the future. Perhaps as a private sitting room just for the family, or a guest bedchamber.

William came back with a basket full of food – ham, biscuits, apples, pecans and a nutcracker. He placed it on the bed, then went back out of the room and came back in with a tea tray.

"I brought some ginger root to make tea for your nausea. Maybe if you drink it after you eat, you won't retch as much."

"I'll try it," she said, sticking a piece of ham in her mouth. "It's a shame a woman has to throw up what she eats. How is the baby supposed to get any nourishment?"

"It's just one of the many miracles involved with baby-making," William said. He took his dressing gown back off and got back under the covers with her.

"Are you disappointed with the way I tried to deny my condition?" she asked him before biting into a biscuit.

"No, not at all."

"Truly?"

"Yes. I understand it's a lot to take in, both physically and mentally. You've not been a woman for very long, and we've only been married a short time, so it's all new to you. I do hope, however, that in the future, you will feel comfortable enough to talk to me about anything and everything. Don't hesitate to let me help you with things."

She stopped eating and realized she had to tell him about her wedding ring. This was the perfect opportunity.

"What's wrong?" he asked. He was always so good at picking up her moods.

"William," she began. She smacked the crumbs off of her hands lightly over the basket and then sat up straighter, crossing her legs. "I have a confession to make."

"What is it? This looks serious." He laid his piece of ham down inside the basket.

"I'm so sorry." She looked up at the ceiling, looking for courage, and twisted the covers with her hands nervously. Looking back at him, she said, "I don't know what happened to my ring."

She looked at his expression, expecting to be scolded, but there was something else in his eyes that she couldn't quite distinguish.

"I've looked everywhere but cannot find it. I fear Sam has taken it. I haven't seen it since that night you brought me the new cape, when you picked me up near the blacksmith's."

"Oh, Ginny. No." He shook his head. She knew he'd be disappointed. Then why did he look guilty? He smiled. "Hold on."

He got out of bed and rummaged in the trunk again, coming back to the bed with an elaborately decorated gift box with a green ribbon.

"You're giving me a gift after I told you I lost my wedding ring?" She was flummoxed.

He continued to smile. "Open it up and you'll understand."

She did so, untying the ribbon and tearing the paper. When she opened the little box, to her dismay, she saw her wedding ring!

Ten

"William! What…why do you have this?"

He took the ring out of the box and turned it so she could see the inside of the ring. It was engraved with words that read, *William and Ginny Forever…1873…All my love.*

"Oh, William! You had my ring engraved?"

She hugged him, not waiting for an answer. She was so happy to see her ring again, so happy he was not mad at her, and so happy that he did such a thoughtful and romantic gesture. She looked at it with her arms around his back, the entwined snake eyes looking up at her happily.

When William had presented this ring to her, he told her that the serpent represented many things, including everlasting love, passion and desire, eternity, as well as healing and medicine.

"Yes, I did. Merry Christmas, sweetheart."

She let go of him and asked, "How did you get this? When?"

"The night you mentioned earlier, when I gave you the new cape. I took it off of your finger while you were putting the coat on. If you had noticed, I was going to give the excuse that I didn't want you to snag the new coat or something."

"William, how could you?" She put the ring on and looked at him earnestly. "Don't you know I was worried sick that I had lost it – literally? I got nauseous every time I thought about it. That was a cruel thing to do."

"Ah, now," he laughed lightly. He took her hands in his. "I do apologize, sweetheart, but I wanted to do this for you. I wanted it to be a Christmas surprise. If you had but asked me about your ring, I would have told you that I had it cleaned or something similar. I would not have had you worry needlessly." His face grew stern. "Yet, since you would rather torment yourself in solitude, this is what happens."

She knew he was right, much as she didn't want to admit it. She looked down at their hands and then back up at him. "You are right. This is the second time I've done this – first with the baby and then the ring. I'm sorry, William. I don't mean to shut you out."

He smiled again and stroked her hair lovingly. "I know you don't. You're just not used to relying on me yet to help you, but you will." He kissed her lightly. "I'm not only your husband, I'm your helpmate. I'm here for you, for the good and the bad. Even when you're scared. We have to be able to rely on each other."

"You are right, my husband." She gripped his hands tightly. "I just didn't want you to be disappointed in me."

"I was more disappointed that you didn't tell me. I wouldn't be mad at you if you really had lost the ring, sweetheart. Don't ever be frightened of me. No one loves you more than I do."

"You're right again. I'm sorry." She let go of his hands and hugged him tightly again.

"I'm sorry, too, that I caused you pain unnecessarily." She could hear the regret in his voice.

"Good," she said behind his back. "You should be sorry." She let go and smiled at him, poking him playfully in the ribs. "Thank you so much, William. I love that you engraved my ring for me, truly."

They kissed lingeringly, and then went back to eating.

"You have spoiled me so much, the coat, the furniture, the engraving. I'll never measure up."

"You're wrong about that." She stopped chewing and looked at him. "You've given me the best Christmas present ever – a baby."

She smiled. "This is our first Christmas together, and in our new house. Two firsts."

"With our first babe in your belly. Three firsts."

"I remember the first Christmas after we first met. You had just broken your betrothal to Madeline," she said quietly. "So that she and Ethan could get married again. I remember how sad you looked."

"Yes, I was depressed, I'll admit it. I seem to recall you gave me something. An angel, made out of paper."

"I had almost forgotten. Yes, I did. I didn't know what else to give you, but I wanted you to know that I had thought about you. The angel was supposed to let you know that you were being watched over so you wouldn't be sad."

He smiled. "I remember thinking that was very sweet of you." He kissed her on the cheek. "Oh, and those cakes. What were they called?"

"Soul cakes, yes! I need some of those right now - they're made with ginger." She laughed. "I helped my mother make those. That was a tradition started in her mother's family." Her smile left her momentarily. "Are you familiar with the tradition of soul cakes?"

"It signifies releasing the soul of the dead from purgatory, I believe."

She nodded. "I remember the first Christmas without my father…my mother fixed a big batch and said they were all for him."

She felt his hand on her arm, and she looked up at him. "I'm sorry," he simply said. "Those were good cakes, in any case." He took a drink of some tea. "By the way, it's snowing outside."

"It is?"

"Mhmm." He chewed up a bite of biscuit. "Has been for some time – ever since I went to get this food."

She looked out the window behind him, and sure enough, everything was getting white outside. "This is cozy. Snow at our new home on Christmas Eve. How perfect!"

They finished eating, and William put the basket on the floor, then handed Ginny a cup of ginger tea. They lay beside each other, naked hips and legs touching, cozied under the covers, propped against pillows on the headboard, and held hands.

"Thank you…for everything," she said, picking up his hand and kissed it. "You're so good to me."

"It's my pleasure. Dr. Harrison gave me a nice compensation as a Christmas gift, in addition to the little bit he already gives me for helping him out."

"That's nice, but I wasn't referring to the things you bought me – even though they are all wonderful. I meant all the things you do for me, taking care of me, your thoughtfulness, your kindness and patience, how you can read my mind and know what I need when I need it, and most of all, your love."

"That's one of the things I love about you, Ginny. You don't need much to impress you."

"I only need you." She laid the teacup down on the table next to her side of the bed, and then rolled over on top of William and began caressing his hair and kissing his face. He responded promptly with gentle caresses, lip nibbling, and appropriate utterances of pleasure. Their kisses became more and more passionate, and finally she placed herself onto him and they loved each other wholly, christening their new bed. Afterwards, fully satiated, they collapsed, until Ginny felt urgings in her stomach that she had not felt all day.

"William," she said, holding onto her stomach. "Could you hand me the chamber pot? I think I'm going to be sick."

He quickly reached over and opened the compartment that held the pot, took the lid off, and handed it to her. She took it and then left the room with it, not wanting to be sick in front of William. When she expelled nearly all of what she had just eaten, including the ginger tea, she felt a hand on her back.

"William, go away. I don't want you to see me do this. It's disgusting."

"Ginny, I'm here for you, through the good and the bad, remember? I want to comfort you." He gathered all of her hair together and stroked her back. "Is this one over?" he asked.

"I think so," she said weakly.

He took the pot from her hands, left the room, and then came back for her, picked her up in his arms and carried her back to the bed. He covered them both up and nestled her against his chest.

"Rest, my sweet. You need to sleep. Your body has a lot of work to do inside, growing our baby."

They both slept a little, and William woke up first, noting that it had turned dark outside. He carefully got out of bed to put more logs on the fire. He put his dressing gown on, as the room had gotten cold while they slept. He looked outside and noticed that the snow continued to fall and had deepened, covering up the carriageway completely and most of the bushes. It was unusual to have so much snow in this area, but they were certainly getting it now. Jonas would have a difficult time getting the carriage back here the next day.

Ginny stirred, and he got back under the covers with her to get warmed up again.

"William?" she said, reaching for him.

He hugged her against his chest. "How are you feeling?"

"All right, I suppose. Is it still snowing?"

"Yes, it's getting pretty deep."

"We should go out and build a snowman." She grinned at him playfully.

"Oh no, young lady. You are not going out there in your condition. Besides, it's too dark."

She pouted a little. "To-morrow morning, then?"

He smiled, despite his concern for her health. "Perhaps a walk. That would be less strenuous."

"All right. That sounds like a nice compromise." She hugged his waist. "Why are you dressed?"

"I got up to put more wood on the fire and got cold, being away from you."

She smiled. "I'm hungry again. How about I put on my dressing gown and we have a nice meal in the dining room at that gorgeous table?"

That sounds nice. Are you sure you feel like getting up? And eating?"

"Yes. If I spew it all later, so be it. My stomach feels completely empty right now. I think the baby is gnawing on my stomach."

He laughed. "All right, then."

She put on her pink dressing gown and her moccasins, brushed out her long hair, and they went into the dining room and ate. William lit the tableside oil lamp, which Ginny carried to the dining room, and William lit a fire in that fireplace while Ginny lit the candles on the table. After they filled their bellies and it seemed like Ginny was going to keep it all down, they carried the lamp to the parlor where Ginny played Christmas songs on the piano and sang while William played the harmonica. He joined her in singing the last song.

"You have a handsome voice, William. How did I not know this?"

"I guess I'm just embarrassed. That's one reason why I pick up the harmonica instead."

"You should sing more often. I like singing with you. We harmonize well together."

She got off the piano stool and headed back to their temporary bedchamber. She came back a moment later with a gift in her hand.

"Here's an early present for you."

"You didn't have to get me anything."

"Don't be silly, of course I did." They sat down on the settee together. "Go on, open it up."

He untied a silk red ribbon and tore the shiny silver paper off of a wooden box about a foot long. Inside the wooden box was a tin case shaped similar to a gourd with a narrow top and wider bottom. He opened the case and was pleasantly surprised at what he saw.

"A stethoscope! Ginny!" He took it out of the box and examined the fine specimen. It was a Cammann stethoscope with an elastic band tension mechanism and binaural ear tubes. "How did you purchase this?"

"At the academy. One of my professors told me he could order one for you. He said it was the latest design, from 1870."

"Yes, it is. I've used Dr. Harrison's, of course, but had not purchased one for myself yet. How did you pay for it?"

"With the money you gave me for mercantile goods. I've been saving a little back each week."

"Thank you, Ginny. This is so thoughtful." He laid the specimen on his lap long enough to draw her in for a deep lingering kiss. "Let's try it out," he said. He put the ivory ear tips inside his ears and put the other end up against Ginny's chest to hear her heartbeat. It worked wonderfully, hearing her tha-thump, tha-thump. "Let's see if we can hear the baby's heartbeat," he said, moving the scope down lower on her belly.

"It's a bit soon for that, isn't it?" she said, though she was smiling, clearly eager.

"Shh. Don't talk for a minute." He listened carefully and moved the stethoscope around in different areas until he thought he could barely detect tiny quick-paced whooshing sounds. He took the ear tips out. "Here, have a listen. It's barely audible."

She put the tips in her ears and sat very still, smiling. "I do hear…something. Is that really our baby's heartbeat?"

"It must be. Unless it's one of your other organs. It's hard to say for sure."

"Let me listen to your heartbeat," she said, moving the end up onto his chest. She smiled again. "That's a good healthy heartbeat."

She gave the stethoscope back to him, and he put it back in its tin case. "This is so nice, Ginny. Thank you, again."

"You're welcome. I'm glad you like it."

As he sat the case and wooden box aside, he said, "I must say, I am happy to see you are being frugal, but no more sacrificing food for me, all right? Not while you're with child."

"Yes, I understand."

"What would you like to name our baby if it's a girl?" he asked her then.

"Hmm, Emily? Like your first daughter?"

He shook his head. "No, she was named after Rachel's mother – it was her middle name."

"Oh. How is she doing? It was nice of her to send us a letter when we wed."

"Yes, it was nice. I haven't heard anything more than you have." He felt uncomfortable talking about his first wife's family.

"What's wrong?" she asked.

"It's just that…I don't want to think about Rachel. When I do, I feel guilty."

"Why? Because you still love her?"

"No, quite the opposite. I never loved her the way I do you, and I shudder to think that if she had lived, I would never have met you. And if I'd never met you, I would've never known what true love was."

"Oh, William." She caressed his cheeks and kissed him. His heart began pounding quickly, fluttering. He still got that way with her. She never ceased to arouse him. "My sweet, sweet William," she murmured.

They had relations in the parlor to christen that room. Then William helped her bathe in the little hip bath with some lavender goat's milk soap, and they snuggled back in their bed under the covers and fell asleep as the snow kept piling up outside.

Eleven

"Look at all that beautiful snow, William! Can we please go out and play?"

It was the next morning, and after they ate a little to break their fast, Ginny promptly spewed hers back out. William had cleaned out the chamber pot from the night before, and he did it again after she finished this bout. She had relaxed a bit – at his insistence – and was now begging him to go outside. She felt silly to plead with him, like he was her father instead of her husband, but she knew he was concerned with her health as well as their baby.

"If you're sure the nausea is gone."

"Yes," she said, nodding.

He still hesitated. "Ginny, you know I don't want you to get sick and you know the reason why."

"Yes, I do."

"So, only a walk. All right?" She nodded. "Get ten layers of clothing on and we'll go out."

She laughed and then put on her chemise, decided against the corset as she didn't want to induce nausea or the vapors, put on a thick wool morning dress with a high neckline, long boots, and finally her blue wool coat.

"Wait, I have more Christmas presents to give you," William said.

"More? William, you're spoiling me so."

He smiled. "You know I love spoiling you."

He walked back into the bedchamber and came back shortly with a big box, neatly wrapped in white paper and tied with a big red bow. She untied it and opened the present, revealing a winter hat and muff made out of rabbit fur.

"Oh, William! These are gorgeous." She put the hat on her head. "And so warm." She put her hands inside the muff and smiled at him. "I won't get cold at all in these. Where did you get them?"

"I got the fur from a couple of the rabbits I had trapped last month. Aunt Patsy cooked the meat, and I took the pelts to Wellington Cross one day last month while you were at the academy. I had asked Jonas and Ethan both if they could recommend anyone who did good work, and Ethan recommended Zeke. He is apparently quite crafted in this sort of thing."

"He certainly is. Thank you so much."

She kissed him as he put on his thick overcoat and bowler hat, and they headed outside.

The snow had stopped, and the sun had come out. It was a winter wonderland outside, bright and white everywhere they looked. Icicles hung from the house as well as on tall grassy weeds nearby, glistening in the sun. They walked towards the river, holding hands. The only sounds were the crunching of snow underfoot and the calling of birds. The smell of firewood from the house drifted in the air.

It was a slow walk because of the deep snow, and quite difficult to keep Ginny's dress bottom from getting soaked. They reached the river, which was partially frozen and more icicles clung to fallen tree branches. A short distance away, Ginny suddenly saw a doe. She touched William's arm and pointed towards the deer, which was staring at the two of them, bright-eyed and looking scared. But she didn't run away. Ginny wondered why. William touched her on the arm and motioned to a little fawn on the other side of them. They stood directly between mama and her baby. Ginny mused about the mother protecting her baby, which was obviously the reason why she didn't run away.

William motioned for them to turn around and head back the way they came, so they wouldn't bother the deer. They slowly walked away, and at the top of a slope, they turned around to see that the mama had gone over to where her baby was and put her nose down at the baby to nudge her. Then she took off running, and the fawn followed her. William and Ginny smiled at each other.

Once they got back to the house, Ginny begged to build a snowman again. "Please, just one snowman, right here next to the house? That way, if I get cold or tired, I won't have far to go to get back inside."

William sighed but relented. "All right, one snowman, and then back inside."

She kissed him on the cheek. "Thank you."

Ginny placed her muff on the front porch, and they started building the main parts of the man, beginning with a small snowball and rolling it around to get more and more to stick to it. William did the bottom part, while Ginny did the middle. When she had hers as big as she wanted it – a little smaller than the bottom one – William lifted it up on top of his. Before they could decide who would build the head, Ginny picked up a tightly-packed snowball and flung it toward William's back. She wasn't a very good thrower, though, and it hit his head instead. Her eyes widened and she gasped.

"Hey!" he shouted, half laughing. "That actually hurt."

"I'm sorry," she said, giggling herself. "I meant to hit your back, not your head." She walked towards him to wipe snow off of his reddening cheek. Before she could reach him, he bent over and then stood back up with a snowball of his own and came at her and smeared it on her cheek.

She screamed. "That's cold!"

She bent down and picked up another bunch of snow and pressed it into a ball and hit him in the chest, as he came up for another snowball, which he threw and hit her on the arm. They laughed and threw more snowballs at each other, until Ginny suddenly felt very light-headed and dizzy. William threw the last snowball before he noticed her change in condition, and she fell into the snow as the snowball hit her on the hip.

"Ginny!" she heard him yell, and then she felt herself being picked up.

William quickly brought her inside the house and laid her on the settee in the parlor. He removed her coat and boots and quickly went into the bedchamber to get his medical kit. When he brought it back, she came to as he was getting out a bottle of smelling salts.

"Ginny!" he let out a deep breath. He lifted her up for a long hug, dropping the smelling salts on the floor. "You scared the life out of me."

"I'm sorry. Did I faint?"

"Yes, you did, and it's all my fault," he said behind her back.

"How is it your fault?"

"Because I let you talk me into building a snowman when I knew better." He looked at her earnestly. "You know how hard it is for me to say no to you. Don't do this to me again."

She smiled faintly. "I'm sorry, William. Truly, I am."

"I cannot lose you," he said, kissing her. "I cannot," he murmured.

He then picked her up and carried her back to the bedchamber and laid her on the bed and began taking her clothes off. Once she was completely nude, he asked her, "Would you mind if I examined you and the baby?"

"Of course not, but I really don't think it's necessary, William."

"Let me decide that." He felt around her lower abdominal area in different areas while watching her expression. "Does anything hurt?"

"No, not really," she said.

He then examined her inside for the mucous plug, which was still intact. He looked up at her, and she was smiling at him, clearly aroused by his examination, but he couldn't think romantically until he was sure she and the baby were safe.

"Do not smile at me in that manner while I am examining our baby," he said, thoroughly focused on being a doctor at the moment.

She giggled.

"Everything seems to be fine. Nothing hurts?"

"Nothing at all."

He completed his examination, noting that he didn't see any blood, for which he was relieved. He placed her under the covers, pulled them up to her chin, and quickly left the room to get another blanket from the parlor and placed that on top of her. He then lit a fire in the fireplace and proceeded to strip all of his clothing off while she watched him, and then he got under the covers with her and nestled her against him.

"This will help warm you up quicker, having our bodies together, skin to skin."

"Is that right?" she said, grinning.

"Yes, it is," he said, still looking serious.

"I am thoroughly enjoying all of this, but nothing hurts, and I'm not cold. I think I fainted because I'm hungry again. I spewed everything out this morning, remember?"

"Of course, what was I thinking?" He wasn't thinking clearly, obviously. All he could think about was how devastated he would be if anything happened to her or their baby. He got out of bed, put his dressing gown on and went to the dining room to get some biscuits and ginger tea and brought them back on a tray. "Try drinking a little tea before you eat this time, see if that helps."

She obeyed.

"I'm only giving you something bland for now, to see if you can keep that down."

"All right. Thank you."

She ate a biscuit and drank some tea and seemed to keep it down. "It does seem to help," she said. "I'm feeling some better."

"Good." William started getting dressed.

"What are you doing?" she asked him.

"It's almost time for Jonas to come to pick us up and take us back to Magnolia."

"Oh," she said, sadly. "Do you really think he can get the carriage here in all that snow? The carriageway is covered up, and we barely know where to go even without the snow."

"Perhaps they can find a sleigh."

"They don't have one as far as I know. Oh, I haven't given you your other Christmas present yet," she said. "Don't put all those clothes back on yet, please?"

He stopped with just his long underwear on. "You got me something else? Ginny, you didn't have to do that."

"Nonsense; it's Christmas. Look in my trunk."

He opened up her trunk and looked around her clothes.

"Look under that blue dress. That's it."

He pulled out something soft wrapped in shiny paper and tied with a dark green ribbon. He untied the bow and tore the paper to reveal a soft, tan-colored handmade something. He held it up and saw that it was a scarf. "Did you make this for me?"

"Yes, I did. Do you like it?"

He put it around his neck. "Yes, very much." He examined the stitching. "Is this knitted?" She nodded. "When have you had the time to do this where I couldn't see you?"

"I've been keeping it at Aunt Patsy's house, and I just worked on it a little each day when you were over in the cottage doing other things."

"Where did you obtain the thread?"

"From Charlotte Clements's sheep. She brought some for my mother, and Mother gave some to me."

"I love that you made this for me. Thank you." He tied it, feeling the warmth and softness against his neck.

"You're welcome. I should have given it to you before we went outside. I was so excited about my gifts that I forgot about yours. Forgive me for forgetting."

"You're forgiven." He leaned over and kissed her on the cheek.

"Now, come lay beside me a little longer before we have to leave our new home," she begged, pulling his arm towards her. "I don't wish to leave just yet. Can't we stay here another day?"

"Would you have Jonas travel all this way through snowy terrain just to turn him away? Besides that, your mother has worked hard on cooking and would like for us to be present for Christmas dinner."

"Oh, very well, then."

William looked inside his trunk and found his pocket watch, saw that the time was half past eleven, and then got back under the covers with her. "Just for a little while. We only have half an hour before Jonas is supposed to be here. How long will it take you to get dressed?"

"We can stay here the whole half of an hour. I promise I'll dress quickly. I just want you to hold me a little longer."

"I can do that." He put his arms around her and kissed her head.

"If he doesn't make it, then we'll just be snowbound in our home." She picked up his hand and kissed the back of it. "There's no one else I'd ever want to be snowbound with than you, my dear, sweet husband."

Twelve

Ginny and William got fully dressed at the noon hour and relaxed in the parlor while waiting for Jonas to arrive. A big sleigh pulled by two horses arrived at The Forest later than expected, but instead of Jonas coming alone, Ginny's mother and two half-siblings accompanied him.

"Mother! What are you doing here? Where did this sleigh come from?" Ginny asked, greeting them at the door.

"Merry Christmas, sweetheart! It's our little surprise. We're all coming here for Christmas dinner," she said, following her daughter into the hall. She turned around and called out, "Don't forget the food, Jonas."

"You're bringing the food here? How sweet. Whose sleigh is this?"

"Ethan's. Jonas rode over to Wellington on horseback, and Ethan insisted. Jonas is taking it back over to get them and bring them here."

"The Wellingtons are coming here, too? How wonderful!"

"Yes. The snow foiled our surprise plans, as we wanted to arrive at the same time, but we all wanted to be together to help welcome you to your new home for Christmas, despite the weather."

"I'm so glad you came here. I was not looking forward to leaving it just yet. No offense, but William and I have been enjoying each and every room." She glanced at William, who was helping Jonas with boxes of food, and she blushed slightly, thinking of their intimate times in these rooms. "Come into the parlor where the Christmas tree is. You and Madeline did such a wonderful job decorating the house. Thank you, so much."

"You're welcome. We wanted to make it look special for your first Christmas together."

"We appreciate the loan of some of the furniture," Ginny said, sitting down on the settee beside her mother.

"You're welcome to use it as long as you need to. How are you feeling?"

"Much better for the moment. William has been absolutely wonderful."

He walked into the parlor at that moment, smiling at her. He must've heard what she said. "Ginny, I'm going to take the sleigh over to get Ethan and the family and let Jonas stay here and warm up."

Ginny stood up and walked over to William. "May I come with you?" She put her hand on his arm.

"Absolutely not. You're not going anywhere. You've already fainted once today."

"Ginny!" her mother exclaimed. "Are you all right?"

"Yes, I'm fine," she said to her mother. She turned back around and looked at William. "Very well, if that is what you want me to do. But don't be long, for I shall miss you terribly." She reached up and kissed him on the cheek.

He hugged her and whispered in her ear. "I'll miss you, too." He kissed her forehead and then let her go. "Stay indoors and get some rest." She nodded. He smiled at both ladies. "I will return shortly."

After he left, her mother said, "Come sit down, Ginny. You need your rest."

Ginny did so.

"I see the honeymoon is not over yet."

"Oh, no, it's not and I hope it never will be."

"I'm glad to see how close you are and how much he cares about you. Is he happy about the baby? I really didn't get to talk to him about it before you came here yesterday."

"Yes, he's ecstatic, but terribly worried about me, of course. He is concerned about me and the baby as both a doctor and as a husband who lost a wife and daughter in the past."

"I'm glad he gets to do it all over again with you."

"Me, too. I am finally getting used to the idea of carrying a child. William has been so wonderful and understanding. I didn't tell you that I hid my suspicions for nearly a month."

"Ginny!"

"I know it was wrong. I am learning to rely on him more instead of holding things in. He has helped me through all of this so much. I regret not telling him sooner because he's taken such good care of me. I have put myself through a lot of misery for nothing."

"It's all right. You're new to all of this. Love is only the beginning of a marriage. There's no guide book to it. You just have to learn as you go, and learn to trust each other and be honest. I have no doubt you two will do just fine, and believe it or not, your marriage will grow even stronger the longer you are married, if you never stop caring for each other."

"I never told you, Mother, but I am glad you were able to start over, too, after Father died. Jonas has been good to all of us."

"Yes, he has. Thank you. I know it was hard for you at first, but you took Jonas right into the family, and I appreciate that so much."

"He's been very kind, and it was good to see you happy again."

Just then, Jonas came into the parlor with a pile of wood. "I chopped some more wood for us. I'll put more in this fireplace. It's really cold out there."

Ginny worried about William being out in it and hoped it would not take him too long to get the Wellingtons and bring them back. In the meantime, she showed her mother the presents from William and told her about a few of the things they'd been doing at their new home.

William urged his horse, Midnight, and Ethan's horse, Blackfoot, through the snow, heading towards Wellington Cross. He followed the tracks already made by Jonas who came up the carriageway before him, until he got to the main road. Here, he turned right and continued following on. The air was bitter cold, a drastic change from the warmth of the house and holding Ginny close. At least he had the warm scarf close around his neck to keep him warm. Her scent lingered on it, making him miss her already.

Ahead in the middle of the road was an obstruction. As he got closer, he saw that it was a fallen tree. He stopped the horses and got out to see if he could move it. He dropped down into the deep snow and trudged over to the big trunk. It was quite large, and he knew he wouldn't be able to move it by himself. He would have to go around it.

He could see Jonah's tracks from earlier, both lone horse and then double horses pulling the sleigh, so this tree had just fallen in the past half hour. He inspected the woods by the road and around the fallen tree, to see if he might maneuver the horses and the sleigh that way, but the trees were too close together. He walked across the road to the other side where the branches of the fallen tree were narrower, and thought that he would be able to lead the horses around that way without too much trouble.

He got back on the sleigh and guided the horses over to that side of the tree. They pulled him slowly past the tiny branches of the tree, close beside some pine trees and holly bushes. They almost made it past when the sleigh slipped on something, and he slid backwards into the holly bush. The prickly leaves pierced his overcoat and tore the skin of his ungloved hands. He cried out from the pain. The horses tried to keep going, but his coat and the sleigh were both caught up in the bush.

"Whoa, steady," he called to the horses.

He patiently removed the stems from his coat and then looked down to see how he might loosen the sleigh. There was more room on the right side of the sleigh, close to the fallen tree, and so he jumped down off the sleigh on that side, only to land his right foot in a deep rut that he couldn't pull it back out of. His boot was stuck. He couldn't see anything except snow, but there had to be a deep track below that his foot had slipped inside like a trap. He tried pulling his boot off, but something was preventing it from coming out, something deep in that snow.

He felt aggravated and impatient. He tried once more with all his force to move his foot backwards instead of up, gave a good yank, but something sharp scraped the side of his boot instead. He shouted out in frustration, which startled the horses and caused them to move, which finally pulled the sleigh out of the bush but caused William to lose his balance, and he fell backwards into the cold, deep snow. His foot was still stuck, and so his knee was bent at an awkward angle on that one side, while the other leg was flung straight out, and he landed hard on his left arm.

Grunting, he looked up to see the horses take off at a trot down the road. "Whoa! Halt! Stop!" he yelled, to no avail. "Midnight, Whoa!" He saw his own horse try to stop, but Ethan's horse wanted to keep going. Disgusted with the whole thing, William lay there and watched the horses carry the sleigh away from him, and there was nothing he could do about it. Hopefully, Ethan's horse would lead the way to Wellington Cross for help. Until that time, all he could do was sit there and wait in the wet snow, and try again and again to get his boot out of that rut.

Ginny was going to be so worried about him when he didn't return soon.

Thirteen

Ginny was in the dining room helping her mother organize the food on the small table. Everyone would have to eat standing up or go in different rooms to sit down when they ate. Her mother had made some wassail, and they placed it above the fire to heat it up. Its spicy scent wafted through the house. Ginny was nibbling on a soul cake, wondering what was taking William so long to get back with the Wellingtons. It had been over an hour. Jonas had already tried to reassure her by saying that it was probably his sister delaying their return, getting last-minute items to pack into the sleigh.

"She probably packed so much, Ethan will have to ride his horse separately," he'd said.

Ginny was still worried, however, and felt a dread in the pit of her stomach and actually had to go into the bedchamber to heave what she had just eaten.

Suddenly she heard the front door open and then close. She hurried into the hall, hoping to see William, but it was Ethan instead.

"Where's William?" she asked anxiously.

Her cousin looked at her. "He got stuck in the snow, trying to go around a fallen tree. He's safe at Wellington now." He looked at Jonas. "I need you to help me move a tree so we can get the sleigh past it."

Before Jonas could respond, Ginny said, "Is he hurt?"

Ethan looked at her again. "A couple of cuts and he got chilled, but he's sitting in front of the fire in the parlor now, and Madeline is cleaning his wounds."

"I'm going with you," she said adamantly.

"Ginny, no," her mother said. "William specifically asked you to stay here and rest. He'd want you to do that."

Ginny looked at Jonas, pleading, "Please, I'll go mad if I have to sit here and wait. I can help tend his wounds. I've got his medicine bag."

"Is there room, Ethan?"

"Yes, I brought William's horse with me for you to ride."

"Very well, then," Jonas told her. "You can ride with me and then ride in the sleigh on the way back. It will be a tight fit, but we'll manage."

"Thank you." She patted his arm and then went into the bedchamber to retrieve William's bag and to put on her cape, hat, and muff.

When she came back out into the hall, she heard Ethan say that they could get another horse from his stables for William to ride if the sleigh was too full, if William felt up to it. She kissed her mother on the cheek, said good-bye to Jonathon and Emma, and followed the men out into the snow.

She greeted Midnight and then climbed up to ride side-saddle, and Jonas climbed on behind her, taking the reins.

"Ginny, we'll take you to Wellington first, get some rope, and then move the tree," Ethan said, riding close beside them. "We'll have to jump the tree. The spot where William got stuck is icy and muddy now."

Ginny nodded and Jonas said, "All right. Hold on tight, Ginny."

They made their way through the snow-covered trees out to the main road, turned right, and then around a bend in the road, they could see the fallen tree and a lot of tracks on the left side of the road where Ethan had been able to pull William out of the rut he was caught in. Ginny shuddered to think of how cold he must have been, lying in the deep snow, which is how Ethan said he found him. He'd unknowingly fallen asleep, but Ethan was able to awaken him easily and help him onto his horse. Ginny clutched the medicine bag and silently prayed that William was healthy and did not have any repercussions from being out in the cold for so long.

William awoke with a start, looked around and realized he was in the front parlor at Wellington Cross. He was lying on a sofa close to the fireplace, and he had a pile of quilts and blankets on top of him. He rubbed his eyes and saw his overcoat hanging over a chair by the fireplace as well as his boots on the floor. Madeline walked into the room with cloths and a bowl of water.

"You're awake," she said, placing the bowl on the floor beside him. "How are you feeling?"

"Cold. Foolish." He was embarrassed to recall how Ethan found him unconscious in the snow. He didn't even realize he had fallen asleep, and that was a real danger, being exposed in cold weather for a long time. He didn't know how long he'd been out when Ethan started pulling him from behind. Once he woke up, he was able to help get his foot unstuck.

"You shouldn't feel that way. I have to say, though, after the initial shock of seeing those two horses coming up the carriageway pulling an empty sleigh, it was quite amusing."

He laughed lightly. "Yes, I'm sure that was a sight to see. It's the same thing I saw as they left me there in the ditch."

"What exactly happened?" she asked as she dipped the cloth in the water. She flipped the covers over so she could reach his hands and dabbed water on the cuts of his left hand first. He grimaced from the cold water and the pain as the dried blood came off. "Sorry," she said.

"Well, there was a tall tree that had fallen straight across the road, and I tried going around it on one side, but the sleigh slid back and got caught on a holly bush. That's how I got these scratches. Then when I got off the sleigh to try and pull it out of the bush, my right foot got caught in a deep track, probably made from a carriage in the past on a rainy day. But something else pierced my boot, perhaps a branch. Is the boot ruined?" He looked at his boots.

Madeline picked up the right one and showed him the damage that had been done. Not a complete loss, but certainly no good in rainy or snowy weather anymore. She put the boot back and finished cleaning his hand.

"I am indebted to your husband once again," William said.

"Yes, well – once again?"

"He saved me once during the war."

"Oh, I didn't know. It's no wonder you're such good friends. And you acted so vague the first time I met you, wondering if I was Ethan's Madeline. You knew all along, didn't you?"

William laughed. "Yes. There aren't too many Ethan Wellingtons out there. It's a unique name."

"Yes, I suppose it is." She started cleaning his other hand. "I'm glad he was there for you – both times. I sent him out to look for my brother, so he was quite surprised to find you out there in the snow."

"I let Jonas stay at the house to warm up. It's very cold out there."

She looked at him worriedly. "Do you need another blanket? You're hands are still icy cold."

"No, I'm fine. It'll take a while for the blood to get back in there and do its job." He flexed and released his free hand. "I can see that you were probably a good nurse during the war," he told her.

She snorted. "It gave me good practice for my own family. I feel like I am a nurse again sometimes."

"Ah, the life of a mother. Did you hear that my Ginny is to be a mother?"

"No! William, that's wonderful! Congratulations! How is she?"

"She's had a lot of heaving and is finally getting used to the idea. She was a bit reluctant at first."

"I imagine she would be, for her first child." She finished cleaning the hands and covered him back up. "I'm so glad you found someone to love. You and Ginny seem very happy together."

"Thank you for saying that. She's made me happier than I ever imagined. What about you and Ethan? Do you want any more children?" He put his hands back under the covers.

"Yes. We're already trying," she said, blushing. She moved towards his feet to clean those wounds when they both heard the front door open.

"William?" he heard Ginny call.

"Ginny?" He turned sharply to see his wife come through the parlor door from the hall.

"William! Oh, sweetheart. I was so worried about you." She rushed over and enveloped him with her warm arms. She kissed his neck, his cheek, and then his cold lips. She put her hands on his cheeks. "You're still cold." She moved his scarf that he didn't even realize he was still wearing up around his ears and cheeks.

"What are you doing here? You should be resting," he said, though he was smiling. He was so happy to see her. He felt better already, just having her with him. He took his arms out from under the blankets to hug her back.

After a moment, Madeline said, "Congratulations, Ginny. I hear you are with child."

Ginny twisted so she could see Madeline. "Yes, I certainly am. Thank you."

William released her so she could talk to Madeline better.

"Thank you so much for all the beautiful things you did for our new house, the beautiful quilt you and Mother made, and for the poinsettia. It's all gorgeous." She stood up and hugged Madeline briefly.

"You're welcome. They're Christmas gifts. We wanted your first Christmas as husband and wife to be special in your new home."

"We appreciate that."

Madeline handed the cloth to Ginny. "Here you go; I cleaned his scratches on his hands, but I didn't get to the one on his foot. I'll leave that to you," she said, smiling. "Where is Ethan?"

"He and Jonas went to get rope to try and pull that tree out of the road."

"Oh. I'll leave you-two alone while I see where the children and Mother have disappeared to."

Ginny turned back around and picked up William's medicine bag she had dropped by the sofa on her way in. "I'll put some witch hazel on these hands and then some salve before cleaning your foot. Are you all right, my husband? Tell me what happened."

As she tended to his hand wounds, he explained to her how he got stuck and how he obtained his injuries. When she finished wrapping his hands, she covered him back up with the blankets up to his neck.

"If we were in our own home alone, I would strip both of us down to nothing and warm you up properly," she said in a low voice.

"That sounds wonderful," he said, smiling.

She put her hands on his face again and began rubbing both cheeks with her hands. "You're still chilled." She then tended to his foot.

"I'm glad you disobeyed me," he said when she finished. She laughed. "I'm so glad you are here."

She came up close to him and kissed him as he put one arm around her back and the other tangled up in her loose golden hair.

"I couldn't stay away when I found out you'd been hurt." She smoothed his hair. "You will not leave my side for the next fortnight. Whenever we get back to our home or Magnolia Grove or wherever we decide to stay, you will not leave me again."

He laughed. "Agreed."

Fourteen

By the time the Wellingtons and the Browns arrived back at The Forest, it was late afternoon. Ethan and Jonas had successfully moved the fallen tree out of the road so that it was passable again, and then they came back for the ladies and children, who squeezed into the sleigh, holding food. William and Ginny rode on Midnight together and Jonas' and Ethan's horses pulled the sleigh, as they all made their way through the snow.

Catherine greeted them when they arrived, helped them all out of their coats, and took food from them to place in the dining room. They immediately started eating their Christmas dinner of roasted duck, vegetable soup, sweet potatoes, cooked spicy apples, goat's cheese smothered in orange marmalade, a pineapple pound cake and a bourbon cake, along with the wassail and some Wellington deep red wine. They took their food into the parlor and ate, taking the two chairs from the dining room and the desk chair from the library, so that they could all be together. Ethan and Jonas let the ladies sit in comfortable chairs while they stood and the children sat on the floor, but Ginny insisted that William sit with her on the settee since he had been injured and had gotten chilled out in the snow. She made him wear extra layers of clothing and also wrapped him up in the quilt that Madeline and Catherine made for them, serving him and telling him not to move.

"You don't have to do this, Ginny," he said when she handed him a plate of food. "I should be the one serving you."

"I insist that you take care of yourself today. You have plenty of time to take care of me later. I need you to be well." She smiled and caressed his cheek. "Besides, I probably won't be able to eat very much before getting rid of it again. So enjoy your food and the pampering."

After eating and after Ginny spewed outside by the back door, Madeline played the piano, and they all sang Christmas carols and Ginny got William's harmonica so he could play that. Her heart warmed as she listened to the lovely harmonizing voices and musical instruments, and even the little ones belted out the words to the parts of the songs that they knew. She looked forward to many more Christmases like this one where her own children would join in the merriment.

It was dark by the time they finished singing, and the little ones started yawning. Ginny offered for them all to spend the night instead of getting back out in the snow in the dark, but they didn't want to impose and there was not room for them all to sleep anyway. So they all made it back to their respective plantations using lanterns to help guide the way.

Instead of going back to Magnolia Grove, Ginny and William decided to stay at The Forest for another week, and Jonas would come back to get them the following week's end. They wanted to spend more time alone while they could, before babies and occupations took a lot of their time away from each other. Therefore, Catherine and Madeline left all the food, and Jonas said he would come back to check on them in a few days to make sure they had plenty of food.

After everyone left, Ginny and William undressed completely, got under piles of coverlets, and nestled together to keep warm. A bright fire was going in the fireplace, and a bedside candle was lit. They talked quietly about the long day's events, kissed often, and talked about their future hopes and dreams, in this house and in Williamsburg. They talked of plans for when the baby is born, planning to come back here to their home for the birth, if possible, and staying for a month afterward. They talked more of baby name possibilities, coming up with Amelia if it is a girl, which was William's mother's middle name, and of course, Liam if it's a boy. They talked about working together in the future, once their schooling was completed, and how nice it would be to see each other throughout the day instead of just in the evenings as it was now.

Finally, they talked about how much they dearly loved each other, how much they looked forward to having children together in the future, and how they would openly communicate everything, even if it seemed trivial. They would find out in the years to come that this Christmas was only the beginning of special memories they would share together and would become a fond memory as a Christmas of firsts… their first Christmas together as a married couple, their first child conceived inside of Ginny, and their first

Christmas in their new home. Ginny would also say that it was the first Christmas she learned to rely on William more and not hold in her fears.

"I love you dearly, William," she said, before falling asleep, her head resting in the crook of his arm, her arm lying across his chest. "Merry Christmas."

"And I love you, my sweet Ginny," he said, kissing her on the forehead. "More than you'll ever know. Merry Christmas."

About the Author

Cheryl R. Lane was born and raised in Tennessee and went to college at East Tennessee State University before marrying her high school sweetheart and moving to Virginia Beach, Virginia. She started writing as a hobby when she was in college after purchasing a couple of Southern Heritage cookbooks, which were filled with pages of beautiful old plantation homes. She wrote more after moving to Virginia Beach and visiting beautifully restored homes in Williamsburg as well as plantations on the James River. She has been working as a medical transcriptionist for over 20 years while writing on the side, and finally decided to self-publish her first book, "Wellington Cross," on Amazon through Kindle Direct Publishing as well as in print through CreateSpace. She has since published book two in the Wellington Cross series, "Wellington Grove," and is currently working on Wellington Cross book three. She is still married to her sweetheart after 25 years, and they have one son and a Havanese bichon dog who thinks he's human.

Made in the USA
Charleston, SC
05 October 2014